Definitions of Love

TASNEEM SARA

First published in India 2012 by Frog Books
An imprint of Leadstart Publishing Pvt Ltd
1 Level, Trade Centre
Bandra Kurla Complex
Bandra (East) Mumbai 400 051 India
Telephone: +91-22-40700804
Fax: +91-22-40700800
Email: info@leadstartcorp.com
www.leadstartcorp.com / www.frogbooks.net

Sales Office:
Unit: 122 / Building B/2
First Floor, Near Wadala RTO
Wadala (East) Mumbai 400 037 India
Phone: +91-22-24046887

US Office:
Axis Corp, 7845 E Oakbrook Circle
Madison, WI 53717 USA

ISBN 978-93-81836-09-5

Books Editor: Cora Bhatia
Design Editor: Mishta Roy

Typeset in Book Antiqua
Printed at Repro India Ltd, Mumbai

Price — India: Rs 95; Elsewhere: US $4

Dedication

I would love to dedicate this book to my mother - Sara

I love you mom with all my heart.

About the Author

Tasneem Sara lives in Ahmedabad and is the director of Wisdom Academy, a unit of Aloha Franchise pioneering in Abacus Education. She freelances for several magazines and writes for the Times of India. The author excels in creative writing and runs an academy for young writers. You can connect with Tasneem through her website www.tasneemsara.com

Special Acknowledgements

I would love to thank my friend Mariam Rangwala, with all my heart. Without her, this book would not have been possible. She is a gem of a person with a creative mind. She has not only helped me edit the book, but also fill the content with crazy ideas that would keep you laughing, long after you have turned the final page. This book is equally hers and I can undoubtedly give her the full credit to encourage me to pen down my thoughts into words that became a story. She is my friend, colleague and guide, and she is the one to whom my gratitude goes…

Acknowledgements

I would like to sincerely thank, Dr. Ila Pathak, Founder Secretary, Ahmedabad Women's Action Group, to guide me along my writing and encourage me.

Last but not the least, I thank all my family members, friends, colleagues and companions who have helped me out to make this idea a grand success.

Love is always patient and kind, it is never jealous.

Love is never boastful or conceited; it's never rude or selfish.

It does not take offense and is not resentful.

Love takes no pleasure in other people's sins, but delights in the truth.

It is always ready to excuse, to trust, to hope and to endure whatever comes.

FOR THE ONE I LOVE

Love is like an ocean,

Deep down the waters run.

Love is like a mountain,

The greatness of which, we got to learn.

Love heals wounds of the heart,

It makes its way,

Love is what I feel for you,

- Each and every day.

Author's Note

There are some faces one can never forget. Three years back, April 24, 2008, I saw one such face. I was sitting in my car, jammed at a traffic signal when he pulled-in beside me in a white Optra. Like everyone around, when you don't have anything to do at a traffic signal, you observe someone who is beside you and that's exactly what I did. He was tall, handsome and had sharp features. When he looked at me for a split second, I observed he had chocolate brown eyes. He was talking to someone through his ear phones. When the signal turned green, we drove into different directions and that was the end of it. But his face had such an effect on my mind that his image came to me over and over again. I imagined what his name would be and there was only one name that clicked my head...

Three years later when I sat to write this book, the memory of his face touched my mind again and I made him a character of my story. I don't know where he is now or what he is doing, after all he was a part of my life for a few minutes only. But if you have chocolate brown eyes and if you drive an Optra, then ask yourself as to whether you checked out the girl beside you at the traffic signal three years back!

Prologue

For me this place was never a Walled City. For me Ahmedabad is and will always remain a city of magnificent malls, broad flyovers and a place hosting a horde of crazy people. Like most of the *Amdavadis*, I can suggest the shortest possible way to reach the SG road, to catch your movie, or can tell you who offers the best *pani-puris* or which jeweller in the city proffers the best designs. I love this city and always will for this place has been a good teacher. It has taught me everything that life has to offer. It has made me experience almost everything, the good and the bad. My mind is assembled with a thousand and one memories of different kinds. Sometimes those memories bring tears to my eyes and at times a curve on my lips. But whatever it is, all those memoirs have touched my heart, indeed very closely. Experience has taught me that in order to judge a person, you have to get acquainted. Acquaintance is possible only when you like a person. You like a person only when you respect him and at times, this respect turns into love. In my case, it most certainly did. Yes, this city has taught me how to like someone, how to respect someone and of course how to love someone.

I stay on the 9th floor of a high-rise apartment, my balcony faces the lake. I look beneath and see people moving, some with families, some with their partners and some alone, like sufferers in silence. I look straight across and I see other homes, painted in beige or white or cream. My thoughts drift, compelling my mind to go and ask them all whether they have married the right person, whether they have got the love of their lives. When I see a woman wearing a dazzling solitaire, one that costs a fortune, which her husband has given her on their wedding anniversary or a man carrying his wife's photo in his wallet, I wish that they really love one another. I think and hope that they haven't made a mutual compromise about which they themselves are even unaware of. As for me, I am madly in love with the gentleman I married to. When he comes home after a long day, I look at his face and come to know whether he had a bad day or a good one. When he takes me in his arms and snores all night, I still feel that he loves me. I close my eyes and feel safe.

I'm lucky that I got the one who loves me more than I love him. Life is crazy. Sometimes love is not expressed by words. When you stay with someone, day in and day out, you don't need to be verbal to express your feelings; your auras do that for you.

Chapter 1

Growing up is fun. After all there isn't a better boon than to sit in the front seat of the auditorium and notice your son or daughter getting graduated, or dressing up your grandchildren for school. Ageing is natural, but it has a lot to do with emotions too. Sometimes you get drained of the routine, pursuing the monotonous chores everyday and performing the duties each and every time. At a certain age, you feel like retiring and let someone else take your place, while you just sit in your arm chair, sipping tea and enjoying the rain. When I grow old, I would want an entire picture gallery in my living room, filled with photographs taken on different occasions. I would hang pictures right from the point when I was in my nappies till the phase where I am attending my grandchildren's wedding. At least, that's what I fancy now. But at that time, things were different, my emotions were yet virgin, for I was ignorant of the fact that life has a deeper meaning besides attending parties, watching movies and checking out the guy next door.

At seventeen, I was still floating in the maritime of immaturity, where the formative years of my life had passed jovially. It was the eve of my 18th birthday, a segment of a lifetime, when I was excited and worried at the same time. Excited because I was looking forward to a great party and nervous because I didn't wanted to grow old. The very idea to accept myself as 18 was something that my mind couldn't take that easily. I wanted all the clocks, for once, to pause forever. Not that I was afraid of death or something, but I wanted to be forever young, like every other teenager wished to be.

To turn eighteen is a big deal. It's a phase when people officially consider you as an adult and the moment you stride in that year, it's like everyone around starts treating you differently. They expect you to behave more maturely and most importantly they want you to start taking responsibilities. I can't say how mature I was at that time, but I had started understanding quite a few things, at least I was at a threshold where I could comprehend what it is to love someone and what it is to be loved.

It was a little before the dusk, the evening drawing close and the last traces of the sunlight seemed to be fading in the bizarre sky. Twilight was my favourite time of the day. With partial light and darkness in the sky, the horizon appeared nearer. The air wasn't that biting, like the way it stings in January. The air was pleasant and cool. My definition for a pleasing weather was the one which would make you fall in love at first sight. I didn't possess a very romantic temperament; nevertheless I was more inclined towards it and during twilight it seemed as if all my romantic instincts would flare up instantly. The evening was busy, like it's always the case with big cities, and since I had nothing much exciting to do, sitting at the back seat of the auto, I was sinking in my self-created notions. My friends told me that I seemed as if I belong to a different world. Not that I had some alien looks with a differed physique and cheesy features, but I appeared more distant, more aloof , as if I am out of place. I would often brood in my own thoughts and it would be after a long time that someone would distract me and bring me back. At times I would get swayed on a wrong route while returning from college, and many a times I would disregard to do important things like locking the toilet door, or turning off the cylinder or taking change of rupees from the grocer. It was not that I wasn't working to assemble my thoughts and live more in reality but the problem was even I wasn't aware, in which imaginary world my thoughts took me.

About that particular evening, there was nothing special. It was the same like every day. But I hadn't imagined even in my wildest dreams that, that particular evening will leave its footprints in my mind forever. All my birthdays were alike. I used to love this day, not because I received a lot of gifts but because I was growing younger each passing year. On my fifteenth birthday, I was excited to turn sixteen. They say that turning sixteen is once in a lifetime, and I wanted to know how that feels, but when I realised there was nothing so special about it, besides it being just an ordinary number, I was looking forward to my eighteenth birthday, because again they said, its once in a lifetime.

Like every year, I was on my way to pick up my birthday cake from the pastry shop. I liked doing that, organise my own party, call up the nearest Dominos and order for the pizzas, arrange for the cold-drinks, choose one's favourite music, wear the best clothes and get flattered. I expected the café to be packed with people, for December is always a season of festivals, shopping fiestas and marriages and even though there wouldn't be any occasion, people here would never want a genuine reason to eat or hang out. They are like those 'happy go lucky kinds' who would demand a treat for almost anything, maybe someone's grandmother's birthday or whether the birth of a puppy. Gujaratis are easy going people; at least that's what the people in other states say. If you display something for hundred bucks, they would ask for it in fifty. If you agree to give in fifty, they would demand it for free, and if you are ready to give them free, they would ask for two.

I was born on December 5, 1988. There may be some thirteenth zodiac for this date, but I cannot imagine myself being anyone besides a Sagittarian. My friends say that I am a example of this sun-shine, the ones who are most compatible with Librans, freedom seekers, adventurous bunch of people and most of all atrociously flirtatious. I did not mind any of the above because these traits portrayed me. Flirting is the most elusive, subtle and effective form of influence that exists and there is actually a very trivial line drawing cheapness and flirting apart. If you didn't know the art of flirting, you may appear a cheap stud. I often tried to analyse myself as per my zodiac sign and I realised that all of it was true. Gradually, my interest in astrology elevated only to the extent that I would follow the guidelines mentioned in the daily paper. If my zodiac told me that my health was sensitive round the week, I would take a little extra care, if it mentioned that there was a fight round the corner, I avoided getting into arguments, and at that particular day, my zodiac said that something interesting was going to happen in life. Actually this was written many times even in the past, but nothing ever happened. But on that day, to be specific it was written, 'spice will be added to life today'. I did not know what that meant, but I had a strong intuition that if it was written, something or rather someone would surely turn up.

I pushed the café door inwards, walked straight towards the counter and without uttering a single word, showed the receipt of the order given. It was a small room, with dim orange lights, black worn out furniture but always boasted of preparing the best cakes in Ahmedabad. Since years I had been eating its cakes, and all I could say that they were yummy. The old man behind the counter was packing the parcels in a steadfast rush. I had been seeing this stout man, since the time I came here, year after year, in the same black suit and white shirt, with the same type of hair style and always wearing the same monotonous plastic smile. It was like, anytime you walk in the café, he would be there. His name was Ramshukla Bhagau and he was one of the most senior people there. Looking at him, I was thinking that some things and some persons do not change that easily, and even if they change your mind cannot accept the altered form so promptly. Like you can't imagine somebody else to be your class teacher or cannot get used to so easily with a new neighbour. This was equally same with the things which you get used to. A new pillow will not give you a sound sleep like your previous one and a new shoe will not only give a shoe bite, but your mind will also take two to three days to see your feet setting into something new.

I was waiting for my parcel while checking out the crowd and to all I could say was that the effort was worthless. It was as if God had completely stopped the manufacturing of good boys in the city. Everyone seated there were like total turnoffs types. It was pointless and a sheer time waste to look at them and have any hopes, so I started observing myself in the main glass door, was thinking I needed a haircut, when just someone pushed the door and marched inside.

When a writer sits to think of a story, and his or her mind finally frames one, it's like 'yes, this is it'. Similarly when a woman goes to buy her jewellery and out of the thousands of patterns laid out before her, she picks the one she likes the best, she says, 'Wow, this was what I always wanted'. I also had the same kind of feeling. When I looked at him, I did not jump like the writer who finally got some piece of his mind, or the woman who behaved as if she never saw a jewel before, but I definitely fixed my eyes towards him and my jaw hung in awe. When you like something, the very first time you see it, you do not tend to forget how it appeared. Like you would still remember your best childhood frock or your favourite toy and how you turned the key to play it, how it made a typical sound and how it blinked its red and golden light. I still remember how he looked that time, and when I recall it all, it seems as if I just saw him yesterday. He looks younger in my memories; truer in my mind, as if he is standing in the café, as if I am observing myself in the mirror, and thinking that I need a haircut, when he just pushes the door and marches inside.

He was five seven or perhaps five nine, brown eyes, like the ones that would remind you of warm melted chocolates, and a radiant complexion. He wasn't that tall, dark and handsome types, one those are described in goofy love stories, yet he carried an air of sheer handsomeness. He was talking to someone over his Blackberry, may be his wife, or girlfriend or whoever and just like me produced the receipt to the cake man. We were standing just an inch apart, I could smell the perfume he was wearing, observe his jaw moving while he spoke; could see the nerves of his neck going down his chest and all I remember that my stomach began to churn. It was not that I hadn't seen or met a guy before. Of course I did and that was the reason I use to look forward to every fresher party at the beginning of the new term and especially during those days use to avoid oily and fried food. The fear of unwelcome pimples was far more than anything that time. It was not that the bloke standing beside me was everything in the world, but yet my senses responded to him immediately. If was as if all my strings got attached to him, and swiftly I had a very funny feeling in my stomach, the one my friends used to call, butterflies. I didn't even realise that I was looking at him, rather starring him when our eyes met and he gave me a genuine, affectionate smile. I could not comment on his smile, for all of it happened so quickly that I was completely taken off guard. For a micro second, I was zapped. I did not even return his smile, like an idiot just ogled at him. His lips were still moving over the phone in a measured rhythm. I wasn't paying attention to what he was babbling but amidst the chaos of the customers, in between the loud music of the café, all I could hear was his soft velvety voice. Meanwhile the cake man broke my trance and handed me the parcel which I very neatly and lovingly carried home.

Chapter 2

Every house has a family and every family has a story. My home, like everybody else, was my comfort zone. I had resided in that house forever, regrettably I couldn't mention since the time I was born, but I admired that house like anything. I had dirtied its floor while playing hours with the clay, had ran in and around it, had talked with its walls and now it was as if the house was like a part of me and all my emotions were attached to it. How much ever bad my day would be, things would feel better once I got home. If I was out for a couple of days, I would start feeling homesick for the house carried such positive essence. I assumed that even my parents underwent the same sentiment and that is why dad never brought up the proposal of shifting elsewhere. In a way, he also felt attached to the house, the way it was, old and ancient and that was one of the reasons why we never planned to renovate it. It was not that we did not like any changes or were diffident to spend, but the three of us were so used to our abode and the way we lived in it, that incorporating any alterations would be like departing from some old family member.

By three I meant, my mom, my dad and myself. Ours was a nuclear family of three. My strong headed, beautiful mother was a physiotherapist at a private hospital and my dad was a true businessman. His heart lied in his wallet. Not that he was a miser but he was a self-made man and valued his assets. I was one of his highly expensive, exorbitantly maintained asset and on the top most of his priority list.

I placed the cake on the dining table and tapped my mother's shoulder from behind.

'How was your day, Anna?', she asked just like every day.

Dad preferred to say Tamanna, but mom always called me by my nickname.

'Always the same, long lectures, boring professors', I said. 'Lame boys', I wanted to add but thought it was best to put a full stop.

'Always the same, bunking lectures, incomplete journals', my dad added while sitting on the dining table. Dad never used to raise his voice or scold me, but whenever he wanted to shoot a hint, he would exploit the roundabout expression of words. In fact, none of my parents ever scolded me in a high tone or had never shown coursed unnerving staggering attitude. Whenever they were unhappy they would just keep quiet and over the years I had become use to that. Silence at home means something was wrong and that is when it was time for me to be more alert or say be in a 'holier than thou persona'.

We were having supper early that night because mom and dad planned to go to watch a Gujarati drama. As such we had our food early in the evening because my parents were very conscious about the diet cycle and all.

'So who all are coming at night for the party?' Dad went on.

'Hmm, Sophia, Maria and Nikhil.'

My throat felt tight whether to add Vikas's name, for I didn't know how my parents would react. Dad was cool but I did not know what mom would say so I purposely skipped his name. Actually talking about Vikas, was like a taboo at home, since once and for all he had led his image knocked off down the drain. A year back, it was a Sunday evening and Vikas had come home to exchange some notes and when my mom had offered him tea, asking what he would like to have with it, some biscuits or snacks, he had coolly mentioned,

'Nothing aunty, tea for me is like neat vodka. I don't like mixing it with anything.'

He was the only one to laugh at his joke, because I didn't even dare to smile and mom had given him one of her dirtiest looks. Perhaps if mom wasn't present there, I would have laughed to death.

After that incident, I was always a bit hesitant to entertain my friends at home. It was like not nipping something in the bud for now. Anyone could speak anything haphazardly and I did not want to create an embarrassment. I had also warned all my friends that if they come home, they should seal their lips, at least till the time my parents were around. Actually their comments or jokes were not at all a problem; it was my parents who were conservative in their thinking. The main reason for that was all my friend's parents were quite young, probably in their mid thirties, while my parents were in their early fifties. Needless to say there was a vast age difference between us.

'But it's not a party dad, it's like cutting the cake, smashing it on each other's faces, accompanied by some birthday bumps and that's all.'

My friends were my world. They were very close to me, not only because we did all sorts of weird things in the college together, but because they understood me to an extent. Nikhil was one of those types who would always have a shoulder ready whenever I wanted to cry and Maria was my oldest friend since kindergarten. Maria, Nikhil and I had done all possible things during our college life. We had tried everything from smoking under the campus bushes to trying every brand of every possible type of liquor.

My parents left quickly after supper. I locked the doors behind them and went into my bedroom. My room was big enough. It was as per my taste and was more of a contemporary style. It was painted in a light shade of purple with a contrast of jasmine white. There was a balcony on its northern side which faced the garden and a bed towards the left. Opposite to it was the dressing area. There was also a study table, which I hardly used for most of the times; I did all my work on the bed. The book shelf was filled with all sorts of fiction books, fashion magazines and fantasy stories which had no connection with education whatsoever.

At night, I had a habit of putting things down in the diary. I used to recall, whatever nice or ugly happened with me since the time I woke up in the morning. I was an early riser, I liked watching the sun waking up; it was a feeling of well-being. I liked making my own cup of tea in the morning; I liked watering the plants, and chatting with the newspaper fellow, the milk man and the vegetable vendor in the morning. My day always started like this, these all things had become a part and parcel of my life.

But that evening I did not consider anything that happened in the morning, or at the college or at home. I was least bothered about all those incidents. That evening my thoughts were focussed only on the guy I saw in the cake shop. I was recalling his style, the way he walked in holding the phone, the way his brown eyes narrowed when he tried to listen attentively to someone on the line, the way he moved his left hand in his black hair and most of all the way he broke a smile at me.

My thoughts took a turn when the clock struck ten and I began piling heaps of clothes on the bed while deciding what to wear. I was very choosy when it came to select the clothes or deciding what to eat or when it was a question of making new friends. At last, I kept everything aside. I took a hot shower, slipped in my pink pyjamas and white t-shirt. I rolled my hair upwards and put a butterfly clip. I wore my pink glasses, picked up a Sidney Sheldon and began reading. But my mind was so occupied thinking about him that I was just mechanically turning the pages of the novel. I was unable to concentrate on anything. For a while I looked at myself in the mirror and my reflection compelled me to think about my mom. I was an ordinary looking girl, with no special features. It was only that I was tall and fair and my small black mole beneath my lower lip was often complimented. I did not want to get upset that night so I packed all my thoughts about my parents in my mental suitcase and shut it tight. I put on some soft music and was standing at the balcony when I thought I saw something. That something was a white Optra parked unusually outside our gate. I looked around but a car at our gate, and that too around 11 at night, was a little strange.

Before I could give it a second thought my cell phone began flashing an unknown number. This was in a way funny and scary at the same time. It was completely similar to the one they showed in those scary serials and for some time I thought that my friends were playing one of their pathetic pranks. But then neither of them had an Optra, nor any of them drove a four wheeler.

'Hello, who's this?'

'Ah, ma'am, this is Sameer Raheja. I don't want to ring the door bell so late night. Sorry to disturb you at this time, but could you please open the door?'

This was all very confusing. I rushed downstairs; jumping two steps at a time and like a fool without peeping in the eye hole, flung the door ajar.

Chapter 3

Winter was the only pleasant season in this city, the time of the year when people would appear more zealous, while in summers everybody seemed to turn passive for the useless 'beat the heat' schemes did not much work here. A week after my birthday, the atmosphere turned colder and the evenings drawn in soon. I always liked welcoming winters, especially because it gave more time to sleep at night. But the long nights and short days made me feel sluggish. December was also a month which passed away quickly and especially when you have exams in January, time seems to fly even more promptly. I completely deem, Einstein's theory of relativity. When you are attending a dreary lecture, even the last ten minutes seem like an eternity. The same thing when you have a night out or watch your favourite sport on the television, it appears as if time is running on a metro express rail.

Time seemed to stop even when it came to seminars. Our psychology department in the college was sort of a 'seminar maniac'. They had this absurd habit of inviting some funny people, whom they contemplated to be geniuses, to make us sleep while they continued to supply loads of unwanted and unwelcomed information. For me, this always, was the best lullaby, the only difference was that here I used to sleep with my eyes open. Whenever I wanted my mind to relax, I used to await a seminar. Our HOD had one of the worst choices when it came to decide the topics. Sometimes they were on teenage problems and stupid hormone balance therapies and at times they were on drug addictions and kleptomaniacs. That day however the topic was 'adoption', the word which kept on haunting me off and on every other day. I had developed a kind of phobia regarding this word, like adoptionaphobia, if such a thing existed.

But unlike those bald, old, salt and peppery lecturers with receding hairlines, this lady was far better. She was sweet, middle-aged with a short feathery haircut, which went well with her facial features. Her name was Dr. Monica Hiwale and she was a clinical psychologist. While taking the seats, we picked the last row thinking to throw peanuts on our studious classmates and also on the one who pretended that they were studious. But in course of time, I found the seminar to be so engrossing that I got lost into it.

Dr. Monica related the problems and detailed psychology of an adopted child and their other relevant predicaments. We were shown documentary clips of few families who went for adoption. Children who are adopted early in their life and who later come to know about it suffer a lot. Such children are at greater risk of developing a disorganized attachment. Those kids who are ignorant of their blood relations suffer an identity crisis and behave in absurd ways. Not that this is always the case, but many times such a situation does exist. Children may become more violent or arrogant by nature or may tend to sink into depression and a feeling of self pity to the extent that they even attempt to suicide. She also told us several incidents as to what happened when the child came to know that he was adopted.

The last part of the seminar was the questionnaire round and to my surprise many students participated in it. The colloquium was interactive from both ends. Several students related their personal experiences or shared incidents about the ones whom they knew were adopted.

'There was a boy who came to know about his adoption when he was twenty one through his relatives. He came to know through his relatives. He was not able to digest the fact and he ended up getting fits. His treatment took several years and when he was okay, he was still not at ease with his parents', Vishwanath said. He was one of my fellow classmates and my partner in the psychology lab. The boy he was relating was his cousin brother who stayed in Delhi. I remembered, once he had told me about this, when we were fooling around the lab, killing time.

Shruti, who was also in our division, talked about a girl, who got to know about the adoption when she was sixteen. This was also through an indirect mode and after that the girl left the house and ran away. Dr. Monica commented that it was very painful for the children to learn the fact from the outside sources. If parents themselves tell them at a certain age, the situation can be controlled and chances of the child undergoing some trauma decreases considerably.

What I didn't know till then, and what I learnt after the seminar was that not only children develop mental problems, but even the parents who plan the adoption require some sittings of positive counselling. This came to me as a shock. I had never given a thought to this before. Just like children find difficult to adjust with the parents who are not their blood relations, in the same way even the parents find it tedious to consider someone else's child as their own kid in the initial stages.

Though I was listening, my mind was simultaneously busy in some other thoughts and I decided to meet Dr. Monica personally at her clinic. I noted her clinic's number and the address and after the end of the seminar met my friends in the canteen. Most of us were in different departments pursuing different courses and so canteen was one place where we made adventurous plans of harassing a professor or duping our classmates, it was our hub where we sat for hours and worked on our future plans. As compared to the classroom, we spent more time in the canteen. But on that day after the tutorial, my friends understood the 'leave me alone' expression on my face and did not bother to question me. I left early from college that day, and did not take the auto. I walked back home, this gave me more time to think and when I came home all I did was went straight to my bedroom, turned on the laptop and typed www.facebook.com.

Chapter 4

How come he was standing at my door step and what was he doing here?

I wanted someone to pinch me hard, so that I could wake up from my hallucination but when he again gestured that affectionate grin, I realised that he was so very real. Sameer was the one who had marched inside the pastry shop, holding his Blackberry with one hand and brushing his hair with the other. He was the one who had smiled at me and I had simply stood before him like a statue, he was the same person who had given me goose bumps and butterflies all over and now he was standing right in front of me, with a parcel in one hand and flowers in another. He had come to give me my birthday cake. Our parcels got exchanged by mistake and I had carried his brother's birthday cake home. He had taken the pain of noting my address from the café and had come to my house so late at night because according to 'Sameer logic', anything could be spoilt, but not someone's birthday.

When I opened the door, I stood gaping at him saying nothing. He was the one who spoke first.

'I suppose you have carried the wrong parcel, Miss Tamanna.'

For a moment I did not understand anything, but my name from his lips sounded almost right. It felt good to hear my name through his voice.

'What?'

'The parcel, it's wrong, it's my brother's cake you have brought home,' he said.

I ran in the kitchen, opened the parcel and saw 'Happy Birthday Aryan' written on it. When I walked back in the drawing room, I realised that he was still standing at the door, for I had not invited him in.

'I am sorry, I should have checked.'

'That's okay, it's equally my mistake. I was so busy over the phone, that I did not realise what I was carrying,' he said.

We did not talk much; there was nothing to talk to. I asked him for tea and coffee but somehow he sensed that I was uncomfortable and so he did not engage much into conversation. He left immediately from the door and by the time I went back to the balcony the Optra was gone.

'Oh my God!' that's what I told myself. My expressions were like as if I had just won a big lottery or was allotted the Miss World tag. If that day I had asked for something else, I would have got that too. Like I said, turning eighteen is once in a lifetime, I was exactly feeling the same.

I didn't know about him, but this mistake was one of the best mistakes of my life. People talk about flukes and co-incidences and that time I felt it to be more real. His warm gesture touched my heart and since then we started sending text messages to each other through the internet. Even though we both had each other's numbers, this mode of communication was more fun.

In my life, I never had a boyfriend, or had never entangled into any relation, yes I had a few crushes here and there but never a genuine one which lasted more than a fortnight. When I was in standard twelve, there was a boy named Aamir in my class, he looked attractive and dressed in an attractive manner. Since everything about him was so very attractive, I got attracted to him and both of us had gone for snacks in a café near the tutorials we attended. But when I saw him eating, all I could do was puke. He chewed his food, with his mouth open, and the very sight of it was awful. He even spoke while eating, and whatever he ate I could literally see his saliva mixing with his morsel of food. I swore to myself, that this was the last time, I am out with him, how much ever attractive he appeared.

Similarly when I joined college, I met a boy, Raul. He seemed to be pretty decent, and also ate with his mouth closed, actually that was the first thing I had started observing in boys then. The way they ate. Raul and I had gone for lunch after college, and all the time, he said was 'FUCK'.

'So Raul how was your school life'?

'Bloody fucking!'

'Did you watch any movie recently?'

'Fuck, no, I did not get time.'

After that I did not dare to date anyone. It was sort of a risk, and my past two incidents taught me how to play safe. I was excited about this whole Sameer thing but at the same time I was a little nervous. Within a fortnight either he would find all this dull or it would be me who would get bored. I wasn't sure that this daily message business was good or not, whether it was going in the right direction or not, but whatever it was, for now I simply loved it.

Through our chat I came to know that Sameer designed houses. He was an architect. I never knew before this that architects could be so very handsome. Until now whenever someone mentioned the word lawyers, realty builders, or something like that, my mind would picture a middle-aged fellow. It was something like till now I used to associate looks with professions, something like actors cannot be ugly or air-hostesses cannot be plump. But this notion of mine washed off after getting in touch with this young, dashing architect. In a way his personality matched with his profession. He seemed intellectual. His talks were sensible and humorous at the same time. At least in that initial phase, whatever he wrote or typed made sense to me. Sameer and his parents worked together, his father was also an architect and his mom was an interior designer. They all worked under the same company name, it was as if creativity ran in their blood. With looks like Sameer, I tried imagining his parents, but I pictured funny images in my mind and so thought the better of it. In just one week's time I thought I knew everything about him and within a week I became a computer savvy.

He asked me out three times in the past week. Though I wasn't busy at all, I pretended to be extremely occupied. It was not that I wasn't excited to meet him, but I wanted to gain some more time to know him a little better. I was completely confident that he will not turn up like those MTV dare-to-date types. I was looking forward to see him in person.

About Sameer, I did not tell anyone, not even to Nikhil and Maria and as far as my parents were concerned, it was totally out of question. I had refrained telling them even the cake exchange incident. Actually there was nothing much to tell. I didn't even know what I felt for him. I didn't want to raise my hopes, but what I did that time, at least at that time, it appeared right to me.

We weren't going out for an actual date or something. It was an informal lunch and I too had dressed very casually. I donned my favourite light blue denim and a chestnut brown top; the one mom gifted me recently on my birthday. I had worn round whoops since they were in fashion then, the one those appear more like bangles instead of earrings and left my hair open for the breeze to play with them. With dark liner that bordered my black eyes, I appeared more presentable. I took an auto and reached IIM road at sharp 1: 30 p.m. I had taken a French leave from college, under the pretext of a headache and it was not more than a minute when he drove-in with his white Optra, wearing a white shirt and black glares and stopped right in front of me.

We drove aimlessly for nearly few minutes, before we decided an appropriate place for lunch. There are several food joints and good restaurants that serve lip-smacking delicacies but when you actually sit to think, nothing clicks in your head. This is something like when you carry an umbrella, it will never rain, but as soon as you step out without it, it pours like cats and dogs.

We made a beeline for a place which had good food and also an exceptionally good ambience. Since it was an odd day, there was a very little crowd in the restaurant. We picked a corner table, one that faced the road and chatted for a while till the menu arrived. While his eyes were on the menu, my eyes were glued on him. I could smell the same perfume the day he had put when I saw him first in the pastry shop. Sitting opposite to me, he appeared more handsome. With a little off-shaved and a ruffed look guys actually appear better and it was after a long time that Sameer broke the ice and started a conversation. He was easy to be with and his company was far more comfortable. After ordering food, we talked a little.

'So who all are there in your family?' he asked.

I told him a little about my mom's profession and what my dad's business was. He keenly listened. I observed that Sameer was a good listener and that was a very good quality. It is said that most people want you to listen to them. When you give them your ears, they give you their hearts.

'What about you?' I asked him.

It was as if he was thinking something. His expression appeared bemused; it was as if he was in some thoughts.

'We are four, including my younger brother.'

'Why did you choose architecture?'

I thought he would sit and explain me what structural designing is, and what are its scopes and how much money-making the profession is, but for a while he just looked at me and said,

'For me, architecture is more a passion than a profession. I like designing houses, Tamanna. When I sit with a blank paper and pencil to make a plan, I pour all my ideas into it considering each house I design as my own home. I see things from the point of view of the inmates. I imagine where the person would like to have his bedroom, which corner the children would want their play room to be or will the wife be more comfortable to have a fridge placed next to the platform or a microwave. I imagine people moving in the house, doing their daily chores, enjoying themselves, feeling happy about the house they live in. Architecture keeps me going; it makes things more live, if you are getting what I am saying.'

I understood what all he was saying or at least I was trying to understand what he was saying. I simply nodded and chewed my food. There was a spark in his eyes when he spoke and his passion for his work was literally seen. We kept the 'mother of formality' aside and ate till we were completely saturated.

I asked him a little about the way he designed the homes and learnt that Sameer designed *Vastu-* compliant houses. He said that this maintained peace in the house and the family members felt at ease. He also mentioned what were his keys skills, what were his on- hand projects and what all did he designed in the past and when he saw that it was all going over me, he simply paused the conversation.

'What?'

'Nothing,' he said with a smile. It was for the first time that I observed his smile, it was a crooked one and indeed very seductive.

Actually the peace of the house has a lot to do with the positions; at least it holds a lot of importance for those who believe in it. Like they say that the temple should be in the north east, and that the house facing the south west is not advised. Rotation of the house inhibits its positive energy and therefore diagonal directions are not accepted in the *Vastu*. The science of *Vastu* focuses on how to create a building that vibrates with Universal Energy. It involves the basics of Orientation, Auspicious dimensions and sacred geometry.

After a while, he thought as if it was his turn and so he asked me. 'Why psychology out of everything?'

'I want to work with children, understand the child psychology. I feel that in this busy world, where both the parents are working in order to maintain a standard of living, the kids are often neglected. Due to this a child suffers a lot; no one is to be blamed because everyone here is doing their duties but what about the kid? Just like a phobia or a fear often remains with a person, whatever his age may be, in the same way the early years of a child is the moulding period of his life. What the child may become, how his personality will be, how he will blossom, all of it depends on these initial years of his life. I can't change everything but I want to at least help out such children.'

He nodded and this was signal for me to go on. I was not very creative in the description of my work but yet I was trying.

'Sometimes parents or adults comment that their child is very notorious, or weak in studies or disobedient, but they forget that there are loop holes in their way of upbringing. These children due to insufficient nurturing although appear normal but on a closer inspection some may be hyperactive or some may be those shy types to which people often refer as introverts. I want to work for such children. I want to help them so that things can be altered and they are again the same lively and bubbly personalities.'

'That's a great thought, Tamanna. I wish you luck for this, a beautiful girl working for a beautiful cause'.

'I can see you flirting' I said.

To this he didn't reply and we both smiled at each other. There wasn't a mirror in front of me but I felt myself blushing.

Our first meeting was relatively short. It was because Sameer had work to do, and even if he did not, on a working day like Tuesday, a person should actually behave as if he has work.

'I don't think it's healthy to chat on FB anymore. If you don't mind can I call you?'

'I'll wait.'

He dropped me again at IIM road and from there I took an auto. For a change, I revised my notes and worked on my journals but later at night I was thinking about the passion thing he mentioned.

Your passion towards anything will do wonders. When a person does his work diligently and passionately, the universe is compelled to respond to his wishes. Things tend to happen faster when there is passion attached to it. Human beings are the products of their thoughts and if that thought is a passionate one, the overall personality will also be creative and enthusiastic. But for this, one of the most important things is to remain in alignment with the universe, to be in harmony and peace with nature.

Chapter 5

I was sitting in the waiting lounge of Dr. Monica Hiwale's clinic and now since my life revolved around an architect, I had started observing all the places with intricacies and interest, which earlier I did not. The clinic was a tiny one, coloured in pink. There were two separate cabins, one for counselling and another for the therapy and in between was the reception desk. The reception area was piled up with thick files stating case histories with the year and dates written on it. I observed the sections vividly and since there was nothing much to do, I was playing in my mind as to what I am going to tell her. I was not at all sure whether I would ever tell this to anyone, reveal what I forever felt. But somehow Dr. Monica appeared trustworthy and reliable. Shortly afterwards, she arrived and I was about to go into the consultation room. I felt a little nervous with each step I took but I was damn sure that she was the only one who could solve this.

'So, Tamanna, what brings you here?'

'Your seminar on adoption ma'am.' I explained to her that I was a junior psychology student and attended her adoption seminar at the university. I omitted the part that at times it was forced on us by our professors.

She had a little enquiring look on her face, but I spoke immediately.

'I am adopted ma'am. I came to know about this when I was fifteen.'

'How did you come to know?'

'My parents are quite concerned about me. Mom thought that sooner or later I will find this out from some relative or someone and they did not wanted to risk that. So one day they sat with me and confided the truth.'

'And how do feel about this Tamanna?'

'I am not sure how I feel but I don't feel free…I don't feel light. The worst is I don't know my biological parents and I want to know them madly. I want to know what is my real identity, what was my past religion, I want to hear from my own mother what she felt when she held me first in her arms, why did my parents leave me to an orphanage? I want to know everything.'

There was a very frustrated expression on my face when I spoke all this and she understood this well enough. When my friends said that I seemed as if I belong to a different world, part of it was true. Sometimes I would imagine how my life would be with my real parents, possible that I might be a one born with a silver spoon, or possible that I might be a roadside dame. I would think that if I would not be here, where I would be. What would my father be like, did he have the same eyes like me, or my eyes were more like my mom? Were any of my habits of having a sugarless tea, or brushing thrice a day would be inherited from either of my parents? I would imagine what profession my dad would be into, he would be an engineer, a doctor may or a mechanic, and what would my mom be like, a home-maker or a school teacher or a beautician?

Later she talked with me for almost two hours and I gave her my case history. I told her about my parent's with whom I stayed, how were they like and how did they behave with me. I told her incidents from my childhood. I told her my likes and dislikes, my nature, about my mood swings and possibly everything about myself. I did not tell her about Sameer, I was not sure what she would think of it but I did relate her sad and happy incidents of my childhood.

As a child I was very fond of eating toffees, and who isn't? But at the same time I also had a severe problem of pinworms which many children have. The moment I ate a lot of chocolates in the day time, I had pinworms harassing me at night and so I thought to work in a reverse way. I thought that if I ate chocolates at night, I will not have pinworms in the day time, because they might go to sleep. My parents did not give me many toffees, only calculated ones, since they did not want me to get harassed and so one fine night as usual I was sitting and eating toffees one after another at the middle of the night in my bathroom. I couldn't think of any other place at that time and so I thought that it was the safest place for my adventure.

That night my mom woke up to drink water and while passing by my room saw my bathroom lights on. She waited for a while but even after ten minutes I did not come out; she pushed the door and came in. There were wrappers of chocolates all over the floor and smeared chocolate all around my mouth.

'What do you think you are doing Anna?' she had said, to which I very innocently replied,

'Eating toffees.'

I was six years old then and when I told my parents the concept of eating chocolates at night, they both had laughed and my mom had crushed me in her arms.

I had many such happy memories with my parents but when at the age of 15, I came to know that they are not my real parents, things started changing. That they were not my blood relation changed my perspective to consider them as my parents. Of course there was no change from their side, they were still the same but I became more formal with them and much more distant. While back then, where I use to tell them how did my day go, showed my dad what I painted in my drawing class and told my mother why I liked that particular teacher more than everyone else in school, the scenario started altering. They no longer knew my class teacher's name, or my exam dates to the extent that they were not even aware of my subjects of interest. For a while my mother had tried to bridge the gap but when things had gone too far, she left doing the efforts and since that time things were the way they were.

Actually things were a little odd. We use to stay with a lot of formality with each other in our own house. When dad came home with a headache, he would not ask mom to make a cup of tea, instead he would go in the kitchen and lit the gas by himself. Similarly when mom wanted to go to for shopping, she would not ask dad, instead take an auto and go alone. And as far as I was concerned, I was totally aloof from them. In a way I felt guilty, it was because of me that mom and dad had stop communicating, it was because of my behaviour that they also got use to behaving like that with another. I felt guilty for pulling them apart. Whether I would be able to come close to them again, I wasn't sure, but I was determined to bring them back together.

Akin the meaning of my name, I had certain wishes, certain aspirations but out of all there was one wish I wanted to fulfil badly. If a fairy came to me and granted me one wish I would tell her only this.

'Please tell me who my real parents are.'

When a person loses his memory, he goes mad recalling his past life, the way he used to dress up, what were his choices, who were his relatives and all but here I was in a situation where I just did not know from where I belonged. I wanted to know so many things and when I closed my eyes and thought about it, I felt myself trapped in a cobweb of self catastrophe. People used to tell me,

'Beautiful name', but the problem was how was I supposed to tell them what the meaning of that word meant to me.

At the end of two hours I was completely empty. I felt lighter.

There were some things which were buried deep in some corner of my heart and that day I again gained a little more confidence in myself. A woman's life is placed from cradle to grave; a spirit of obedience and submission, pliability of temper and humility of mind are required from her. After meeting Miss Monica, I knew that I bear all these qualities; the only thing that was required was to bring them out.

Chapter 6

Our second meeting was even more casual than the first one. We had gone for dinner the second time we met, and it was almost after a fortnight since we first had lunch. There was still that excitement to see him and talk to him. Actually I was unable to talk to Sameer or text him all the while. We had decided specific timings and only he used to call me only at that time. Unlike other couples, we did not stick on the phone in the night before sleeping; in fact we never spoke at night at all. I found this a little strange but I never pushed him to talk to me. I wanted him to take his own time and I wanted to give him space.

'Fifteen days is too short a period to dominate someone,' that's what Maria had told me during our English lecture and we both had giggled secretly.

For my second meeting, I had dressed up glamorously. I had worn black denims and a light pink jazzy top, the one that appeared to be a little shimmering. I had also worn slight perfume and a pink shaded lip gloss to add to the effect. Sameer had turned up to the meeting in his best bib and tucker. He was dressed casually in blue denims and a stripped t-shirt. We had gone to eat Mexican food in an open restaurant, a little far away from the city. It was towards the end of December and it was cold , but still pleasant.

This time we did not speak about his work and his office, or my studies and my college. We were both in a light mood and both us didn't want any heavy or philosophical discussions. Although it was our second meeting, we had become quite friendly and open and so I asked him,

'Did you have any girl friend in the past?'

'What makes you think I don't have in the present?' he said.

His answer completely caught me off guard and for a minute I didn't even smile or react. He looked at my expression and laughed out loud.

'Let's not dig the past', he said.

'What about you, have you ever fallen in love?'

'Not till the time I met you', I said. It was my turn to laugh this time and he was pleased with my answer.

'I can see you flirting,' he said with a crooked smile.

'Did anyone tell you that you have the best smile in the world? When you smile, you look notorious.'

'Really', he smiled again and when I saw him doing that, it was as if I my heart skipped a beat.

Sameer came from a well-to-do and intellectual background. All his uncles, aunts and cousins were into some or other gray profession. One of his uncles was a famous and the city's best cardio-surgeon. They were originally from Delhi, but Sameer's father had come to Ahmedabad years back and had settled here before he was born. His brother, Aryan looked much like Sameer and was very close to him. He was studying outside Ahmedabad, in some engineering college.

That night after dinner, we went for coffee. Sameer's car was very cosy and since it was very cold we sat in the car itself and placed the order. It was too early for anything but I still felt like kissing him. I didn't know about the way he felt for me, but that night, if he would have asked to kiss me, I would not have said a 'No'.

'So what else, what are you doing this weekend?' he asked.

'Nothing much, what do you have in mind?'

'Can we go out then?'

'Sure.'

By the time we finished the coffees, it was getting late, and I didn't want any calls from my place, so I asked him to drop me home. Sameer started the car, took my hand and placed it on the gear. He then placed his hand on top of mine. He did not ask for any permission, he simply did that and his act was authoritative. I was shocked and surprised at the same time. One may never know what it feels by first touch; the proof of the pudding is in the eating. Before this, no one had ever touched me so intimately, and I felt really good. Until now, whenever I saw Sameer's messages, or received his call, or met him, I had butterflies, but now when he touched me, I felt as if all the butterflies in my body were dancing on some hard rock music.

'Anything wrong…you all right? Why are you so warm?' he asked.

'Nothing, I just felt very good.'

While driving back, we did not have any conversation. We had already talked too much, so both of us kept mum and took pleasure in each other's touch.

That night I was thinking about what Miss Susan had taught us about touch therapy and tactile communication. The way Sameer had placed his hand on mine, all of a sudden, the way his facial expressions were, all this suggested only one thing; he certainly did like me a lot. But then he never said anything about it. If he liked me, he would have a least told me that, anytime while dinner, or while having coffee or while driving back home, but he did not. Yet another point was, if he did not like me or my company he would not have asked me about the weekend. I was bewildered. I was in two minds that night and both the minds were arguing on something that wasn't required. Finally I tried to sleep but it was not until 2 o'clock that I closed my eyes.

I thought it was high time that I tell Maria and Nikhil about Sameer and so next day after college, the three of us sat in the football court and I told them everything right from the pastry shop to yesterday's dinner. I did not mention anything about that hand placing incident, because even though, Nikhil and Maria were close to me, we had never before discussed such topics. Certain talk, I felt, to be my sole possession. To my tale, both of them reacted differently. While Maria was enthusiastic about the whole thing, Nikhil kept quiet. He did not react.

'I find it a little odd,' he said.

'Now what on earth is odd?' Maria asked him before I could speak.

'I don't know.'

Nikhil was a person who did things based on his instincts. He often talked about this gut feeling and sixth sense but most of the times, what he said never happened. This time also he reacted as if Sameer was someone all together from a different planet. But Maria and I did not bother about it; we kept on talking about Sameer for a long time.

Chapter 7

We were a happy bunch of five. Though I was more close to Nikhil and Maria, I equally enjoyed Sophia and Nikhil's company. Maria and I were in psychology, while Nikhil, Sophia and Vikas had opted for biotech. All my friends were quite notorious and fun-loving. All of us had a common trait to live life in an easy way; actually we were so used to this kind of living, that we never completed our assignments till the morning of the submission date, or at times we prepared for the wrong paper for the sheer laziness of checking the time-table twice. College had made us so lazy and easy going that I found myself completely different in college than back in school as far as academics was concerned.

'You should concentrate on your studies,' I told Vikas one day when he met me in the canteen after he dropped his girlfriend home.

'Look who's talking,' he said and laughed uncontrollably.

Since we all sailed in the same boat, we stood as support pillars for each other. Whenever we wanted to go out with our respective partners, one or the other friend's name was always in spare.

'I am going to Maria's house. I'll be late,' Sophia had one day told her mom and she completely forgot to mention this to Maria.

Actually Sophia's mom had her doubts since many days and that day she had called up at Maria's house indirectly and had dug the truth. The result was that for another fifteen days, Sophia was locked in home, and was only allowed to attend college, that too her father used to come and pick her up from college.

Not only this, Nikhil stayed as a PG in a two bedroom apartment, which was supposedly given to five boys. But these guys shared it among fifteen and the money that was saved, went in buying Vodka, whiskey or Rum or it was spend on the girlfriends. And when any one's girlfriend visited the apartment, the guy used to get a separate bedroom out of the two, and the rest fourteen boys snuggled besides each other in one room. If Nikhil's father had any notion of his son having a purple hair-coloured girlfriend, who wore a nose ring and circulated a chewing gum in clockwise rhythm, his father would have chucked Nikhil's name out of the will.

It was not that Maria did not have any black list stories; it was only that she did things very silently.

'Still waters run deep,' I used to tease her.

The thing was Maria only opted for calculative risks. She tried drinking but when it came to smoke, she refused, saying that it could be addictive. It was kind of true. Similarly, she had her own calendar ready where she had written when she last bunked and now when is the due date. She bunked only certain amount of calculated lectures. Maria's parents were extremely clued up about college activities as both of them were ex-Xavierites, and had an exceptionally good rapport with the principal.

'If anything happens wrong, or if you misbehave; consider it to be your last day in college. None of us are going to come and write an apology note,' her father had mentioned that to her very strictly on the first day of the college and since her parents were quiet firm, she never dared to cross the lines.

When it came to me, even though I was a very quite dame, who did her work neatly, who went to attend religious ceremonies and social functions, nobody except my friends knew the second half of me. There was a devilish side which I possessed and I used to be one of the most notorious characters back in the school and even in the college.

Our vice principal, was a very rude man, with one of the most repugnant faces I had ever seen. He used to roam around the college premises, caught every student, who was on his cell phone, or was talking with some other friends in the corridor, or was chewing something near the library or even sitting and reading near the laboratory. According to him, each student should be in his or her class all the time while they were in college.

'I think he will punish me if I breathe outside the classroom,' I told Nikhil one day.

This man had a habit of going for a morning walk, in a nearby garden near the college and we knew that well. We also used to go there and from behind threw stones at him. We specially picked up big sized strong pebbles, one that hurt more and used to shoot at him from behind the bushes. When he realised that this happened a lot very frequently with him and was not able to find out how, he stopped going for the walks. He started walking early mornings in the college campus itself.

Similarly, on Teacher's Day we used to buy only two big chocolates and gave it to all the teachers simultaneously.

'Happy Teacher's Day,' I told Miss Ketki, and offered her two big Dairymilks. While Miss Ketki left her cabin to attend a class, we sneaked inside and stole those chocolates and gave it to yet another professor.

'This is for you, sir,' and after the sir left the chocolates on the table, they were stolen and given to yet another professor. At the end of the day, the two chocolates were savoured between the five of us and while eating we used to recall each professors expression when they received it and how mad or confused they would get finding those damn bites.

People said that life has a rule. You have to balance everything. The more you laugh today, the more you cry tomorrow. I did not believe in that theory for in my college days, life wasn't that complicated and my relation with my friends, were not knotted with ropes of formality.

Chapter 8

With each session, I became more and more comfortable in Dr. Monica's company. She was the kind of doctor who would make you feel at ease. It is very important that doctors should be friendly with the patients; else one does not feel secure. Dr. Monica was the one, that whenever I saw her face, I felt calm and good. She had that serene look on her face, looking at her I felt wonderful.

It was my fourth session with her. Till now I had told her everything, all pros and cons of my life. She used to often give me small assignments like observation tests and at times to write few lines on myself or my parents. She had also suggested me certain books and movies, which she insisted I should to watch. It was because of her regular assistance that I started discovering more about myself; I had started analysing my behaviour with my parents and friends. I realised that apart from being timid and timorous, I carried a persona of a true feminine genius within myself. I was introvert, but bold; I was sensitive by nature yet independent in my thoughts.

'So Tamanna, do you feel, any better now?' she asked me in the fourth session.

'Very much, the sessions have really helped me.'

Whenever I went to her, the first few minutes she asked me all general questions about my home, parents, my college, studies and most importantly about my friends. She asked about my college professors and friends, so precisely with exact names, as if she knew each one of them personally. I wondered how come she remembered everything about every patient she attended. This time I was going to tell her about Sameer. Since she was counselling me, I thought I should tell her everything. Secrets won't help me in this case.

'What do you feel about your parents Tamanna?'

'I feel that they love me a lot. I feel that they have brought me up wonderfully and that they have taken great efforts and pains for it.'

'Exactly, your parents take a lot of care about you. Have you realised Tamanna, that you and your parents have a lot of age difference? Yet they try to adjust to your way of living and your way of thinking. This is a great thing actually. Although they are conservative, they give you enough liberty in everything. From what you told me about your friends and all, I feel that you have a very liberal and at the same time a very homely background.'

I was trying to sink in what all she was saying and she was saying the truth.

'Tamanna, now you will have to try to make changes in yourself. Talk to them, don't keep any hitch. Try to communicate, tell them everything, what all you do in the day time, tell them about your friends and college. Be frank and open to them. Make them feel that you are comfortable with them. Communication is the best way; don't show them that you love them, tell them by words.'

Later I told her about Sameer, how we met and all, but I omitted the parts I wanted to. I guess even she knew that I told her partially, but she didn't push me.

'Why do you like him so much?'

'It's because, he makes me feel good. I wanted someone elder to me, who would listen to me. Since the time Sameer has come into my life, I do not feel lonely.'

'Does he know everything about you?'

'No, not yet.'

'Good,' she said. I did not quite understand why she said that, but I did not ask her.

With that I completed my session and as soon as I was out of the clinic, I dialled Sameer's number and we met for the evening tea.

Ahmedabad is very famous for its *Kitli* culture. You will see a tea stall at every nook and corner, all of which will be doing fairly well. There will always be a lot of people there, any time of the day. It is like these *kitlis* are the meeting joints especially for students and people from sales. Not only this, if you visit someone's house and say no for tea, it's as if the person would feel offended. Even I was very fond of tea. I would never say NO for it, whatever season or time it was.

'You are glowing, how come?' he asked.

'Because I met you sweetie.'

The actual reason was that after my doctor's visit I was feeling really good. I knew I had to tell Sameer about this, but that day I was not in any mood. I wanted him to know everything right from the start. I wanted him to hold my hands when I was talking to him about it and feel what I was feeling. If I would have started that day, it would have been a long process and after spending two hours at the clinic, I was not in a bit of a mood to repeat the sequence. Sameer had to go to visit a site and I had to lock myself to sit and study, for exams were right around the corner.

It was for the first time, that Sameer had worn a bright orange shade of a shirt.

In my opinion, it appeared a colour of some political party. I did tell him that, to which he just rolled his eyes.

'My...'

Before he could complete the sentence, his cell phone rang and he excused himself for a while.

I sipped my tea and played Tetris on my phone till he finished. I looked at him and thought about the time when we first met in the café. Like this only, he was speaking to someone then, moving his lips, narrowing his eyes, brushing his hair now and then. But the only difference was at that time, it was just our eyes had met for a second and he was stranger to me. Now our hearts had found each other and he was not a stranger to me anymore, but my world.

When he was done with his talk, he seemed a little disturbed and a little angry too. Before this, I had never seen Sameer getting angry; I saw this side of him for the first time. It seemed as if he had some arguments with someone over the phone.

'Something wrong?'

'It's okay, a little matter at home, that's it!'

'Your face shows as if a frustrated person has just fought with his girlfriend,' I teased him. But he was in no mood for jokes and did not entertain it.

I looked at him and waited for him to speak more, but he did not tell me anything.

'Come I'll drop you home.'

Without a word ahead he dropped me home in another twelve minutes.

Chapter 9

That weekend Sameer had asked me to meet him early in the morning around 6:30. He did not tell me where we were going; he said it was a surprise. I told my parents that it was Nikhil's football match, I was going to watch. There was a Jain temple, just a little away from my house and Sameer always picked me up from there. I did not want him to come right till my society gate. Any new face around would incite gossip and I did not want to entertain that. He had worn a sky blue t-shirt and it was for the first time I was seeing him, so early. Otherwise we only met in the afternoons, after my college or for dinners.

From the route I understood where we were going. Once again he kept my hand on the gears and placed his hand on mine. This time, I was not surprised; I was mentally prepared for it

'You look more beautiful in the morning,' he said.

We parked the car and walked for inside. It was a lovely morning and the sun was just about to rise from the horizon. I couldn't say that I ever saw such a beautiful scene before. I might have, but with Sameer beside me, it made all the difference. The sunrise seemed wonderful and with each second, as the sun rose up, the water started to glow. We were standing at the Kankaria Lake and were watching the sun going up. Sameer had held me by my waist, very close to him and I never wanted that moment to end.

'How does it feel?' he asked.

'Wonderful,' I said and knew that he would say, 'just like you', and he did.

We were both quiet for some time as if we both wanted to be alone, yet together. After sometime, Sameer spoke.

'You know Tamanna, one should do this often, not because it's a lovely sight to behold but it's good and important for health.'

'Why healthy?'

'We should take some time out for ourselves too. It is good to be alone and quiet sometimes, it is good to see the sun going up, or coming down; it is good to go for long walks, leaving the vehicle behind. Sometimes, it is healthy to listen to the birds, or watch the world while you sit in your balcony.'

'Hmm, I will remember sir.' I grinned.

After that we had breakfast at a nearby stall and talked here and there about several things.

Sameer and I were very different individuals. We had a lot of dissimilarities, not even in the way we carried ourselves but also in the way we thought. One fine day, while sipping tea, we were discussing as to how the generation gap creates hurdles, may it be father and son, mother and daughter or a boss and an employee. In my opinion the younger one should always obey the elders; at least that was what I was taught by my parents and also in my moral science classes in school. But Sameer believed differently. According to him, the younger generation is more energetic and at the same time more stubborn.

'The younger generation will do what they want to do. It is the oldies who will have to understand and compromise. They will have to bring a change in their thoughts,' he said.

Yet at one other time, we were talking about the clothes that girls wear to college and otherwise.

'One shouldn't wear short or revealing clothes in public, what do you say? Ahmedabad is still not that forward in this. The crowd stares at you in a weird way,' I said.

'No in my opinion, you should wear whatever you want to, but you should feel confident about it and you should be able to carry it. Your clothes should make you feel good and happy. That is more important,' said Sameer.

Although both of us had different opinions we never argued on it. In a way we respected each other's thoughts. One of the reasons why I liked Sameer's company the most was because we use to often discuss such 'out of the blue things', like man travelling to the moon, or a black cat crossing the road or at times why most middle aged females are attracted to young guys. With Sameer, the discussions were always healthy and since he was humorous, he use to come up with really funny examples to justify his opinion. His talks not only made me laugh when he use to say it, but I use to laugh even when he would not be around, say at odd places like exercising in the gym, or while attending a serious seminar or at times while having supper at home with my parents. This was what I liked about him. It kept me going; it was as if Sameer was always with me. Wherever I went I carried his thoughts with me.

With the passage of time, our meetings became more and more causal and then there was a stage where I did not even bothered, what I was wearing and how was I looking. All what mattered to me was to meet him.

Whenever we arranged to meet, Sameer was always on time and he used to never cancel his plans. After my last paper we were suppose to go for a movie. He had made special plans that day. I had to meet him at the cinema hall around 1 p.m. I was already late and so I asked the rickshaw driver to drive fast. When I reached there, I waited for him for almost 20 minutes. I called him several times but each time he cut the phone. After

20 minutes, for what seemed an eternity, he called me saying that it was not possible for him to come. He had to go to one of his relative's place and it was not possible to cancel it. I was so angry that I cut his phone right there, took an auto and drove back home. I was expecting him to call me, but there was no call or message from his side. I kept on seeing my cell phone screen every minute but it displayed nothing. Around 5 o'clock in the evening when my phone rang, I knew it was him and I had also framed dialogues as to what I will tell him. But to my disappointment, it was Nikhil. He had called me to tell me how his stupid football team, had won a stupid trophy. There was no call from Sameer's end that night and I was only growing restless every minute.

I did not feel like going to college the next day. We had all the boring lectures followed by a practical session. When I finished it and was heading outside to catch an auto, Sameer was standing at the college gate. I saw him but did not say anything. He came to me and smiled, as if nothing at all had happened.

'Come, let's go out,' he said.

We went to have a pizza and it was only he who was eating.

'Why are you not eating?'

It was at that time that I lost my temper. I shouted at the top of my voice, without caring what others around would make out of it.

'Don't behave as if nothing has happened. You cancelled yesterday's plan and when I cut the phone you did not even have the courtesy to call me back and now you are sitting an having a pizza as if everything is okay?'

'Tamanna, you were very angry that time so I did not call you back. There was no point to call you back, you would not listen and that did not make sense. I wanted to talk to you and explain you when your anger cooled down. And I did not cancel the plan purposely; there are situations when one cannot avoid certain things. I have a family, which I can't avoid.'

'You are talking as if I don't have a family. Even I cancel plans with them, just to be with you, just to meet you and you really don't care and value it, do you?'

Sameer smiled and said, 'You are still a kid.'

'How can you laugh in such a situation?'

'Oh sorry we are fighting,' he said.

We both kept quiet till the time he finished his pizza.

'Okay, I apologise, now when can I take you for the movie ma'am?'

It was not very difficult to forgive him, for my love was more strong than my anger and while driving back home we prepared a fantastic movie cum dinner plan.

Chapter 10

You would not get sleep only in two situations. Either you are stressed out or else when you are in love. I wasn't sure I was in love yet, but stressed out I really was. More than a month passed away like that and I had to prepare for my final exams. The worst part was, I could never study late at night, neither could wake up early in the mornings and so I use to finish my entire syllabus much before the exams were due. This time, however, I did not blame Sameer for my poor preparation, at the same time his existence in my life had deformed my time-table completely.

I had visited Dr. Monica also only once in the past fifteen days. Last minute preparations, vivas followed by practicals, journal completion and submissions did not spare much of my time. But I had planned to meet her again once I could take some time out.

I never expressed my views to become a social worker and serve children to my parents or anyone else. They didn't force me into any profession but they expected me to complete my PhD degree and open my own clinic. I thought it was time to tell them, what I had planned for myself. I was very well aware that it would come to them as a shock that after my bachelor's degree I wished to put a full stop to my educational career and join an NGO.

Sameer was six years elder to me. In a way it was good. All my friends were of my age and I wanted someone elder to me to look after me, understand my emotions and support me. Sameer never mentioned anything about settling down and still in such a short span of time, neither did I, had any thoughts regarding this. Marriage was a distant dream. It was not that I had never thought about getting married but I had kept my thoughts restrained as far as the wedding topic was concerned. I was not sure what kind of man I wanted in my life and at that stage it was too early to think. My near dream and plan was only and only to work for the betterment of children in the society.

I liked transparency in any relationship, this I learned at a very early age of fifteen when I was informed about my adoption. Since then I was open with my friends and my family. By open, it did not mean that I wanted people to come and tell me everything they did or thought, but I wanted any relation of sisterhood, friendship or companionship to be free, where there are no unnecessary secrets. As far as Sameer was concerned, I had yet not told him about my real parenthood. I had long serious conversations to do with him as well as my parents, but I wanted my final exams to get over, so that things wouldn't get disturbed.

Another thing I hated was a lie. I had my own perspective of analyzing a lie. To lie, means to hide the truth and this word in some situations could be very diplomatic. Lies are often told in two situations. One in which you are protecting yourself and second when you care for your own self. When you go out with your boyfriend and tell your parents that you got late because the professor stretched the lecture is a bad lie. This was what I was doing off lately and the frequency of my bad lies had increased a lot. When you are at some distant place away from your family and in real trouble and you don't want anyone to worry; you tell them that you have severe cold because you ate a lot of ice-cream last night while actually you are crying, is a lie for good. You don't want them to feel helpless. I hated the bad lies and appreciated the good ones and in my opinion the worst possible lie to tell is while playing with someone else's emotions.

My parents thought me to be a very independent creature. But most of the times I had to take support of the good lies. I had spoken ample of bad lies but I knew I was a good person. The bad lies whatever I had spoken was never to hurt or harass anyone.

Like this I had many things on my mind. I had many things to tell my parents and in turn wanted their full support and suggestions. I had many things to tell Sameer and vice versa wanted to hear many things from him, but before I had time for all this, he had to leave.

Chapter 11

When a girl and a boy are in love, there are many facets to it. There is a chain of infatuation attached, where one simply cannot resist blushing while looking at another, there are feelings of care and childish love involved where one would look upon her beloved as a small kid and pick up a parental attitude. Yet one facet of it is the physical urge that both of them constantly feel for one another. Since the time, Sameer had placed his hand on mine, in the car, it was impossible for me to restrict my fantasies. I would imagine him, kissing me at the back seat of his car, or playing with my hair while going for a long drive. And to add fuel to the fire, he had not only held my hand, but also held me very close to him, while watching the sunrise. To be honest with myself, I liked that sunrise not because the sun appeared pleasing, but because I could sense him so close to me. That was one of the times I had controlled my physical emotions from stirring up.

I had heard that girls mature faster than the boys, but I wasn't able to judge how Sameer felt, when I was close to him. But one thing I was sure, that he felt good, I had seen it in his eyes and moreover if he did not feel nice, he would not have instigated the feeling. Certain things happen, only when their time comes and its best to go with the flow. It was not that Sameer and I had never discussed about sex, but we had never planned it between us. I knew something would happen between us, but it will happen in a span of four months, I did not know.

It was a bank holiday and Sameer was supposed to show me his office that day.

'I want to see where you sit and design people's homes,' I had told him.

'It's nothing that great Tamanna, it's just an office like any other commercial place.'

'No, whenever I try imagining you working, seated in your chair, wearing formal clothes, talking over your Blackberry or discussing a plan with someone, I simply cannot visualise. For that I want to see how your office is.'

Since I had insisted so much, he had taken me to show the place. It was actually one of the simplest offices with plain cream walls, two long curved desks and two black chairs. There was long slim cupboard in between the two tables, where I guessed nothing would ever fit and when I saw it, my expressions were as blank as the place.

'What, not your types?' he asked.

'Where are the files, where do you keep the paper work, storage? I mean this does not look an office.'

'Tamanna, we stay in a compact world now. All my projects, paper work and everything are through the internet.'

He was right. Everything was so compact now. It appeared as if the world was small. I met Sameer in the pastry shop, and then at my home and after all even our affair started through the internet. That day I showed him my diary where I used to pen my thoughts. I did not show him what I wrote. But I had a list of dates which I showed him and asked him to guess. I had a queer habit of putting all the lovely dates, the ones when something good happened; the ones which I wanted to remember all my life, in red. And the days which I hated, those dates I wrote in black.

December 6, December 15, January 2nd…and so on it went. All those dates were when Sameer and I had met; I had penned them down in red.

'So now add today's date too in red,' he had said holding me very close to himself, so close that even the passage of air was difficult through us. That was the first time when he had kissed me and we had been so intimate. I had never kissed anyone before this and so I never knew how it feels when some put his soft lips over yours and expresses his love. There was no full stop after that. All my clothes had automatically gone and I was lying down with the man I loved the most in this world. Sameer was a very nice kisser and it was as if he knew where to act and when to act. He worked on the right chords of my body as if he knew what I wanted and by the time we finished making love, I was all together a different person. All I could say was I felt good, it was as if I had left a child within me, far away and had transformed myself into a girl. At the age of eighteen, I did not felt as a young girl, but after this, I felt more juvenile as if the adolescence within me is shouting to be at its peak. After that incident I felt complete and it just increased my love for the person who just before few minutes had come within me and made me experience a different kind of emotion all together.

Chapter 12

It had been four months that Sameer and I were together and even though four months is not a big stretch to time, it is still a long span to get emotionally attached with someone. In the past four months, my life had changed considerably. I had now started seeing new dreams, built up new aspirations and gave birth to new desires. I was not building castles in the air. This difference in my life had come, because of love and care. Love is a powerful emotion, it not only controlled and regulated my life, but it also assured me a happy future. In these four months of time, Sameer had become one of the most important persons in my life. Though we never talked of anything about love, I knew that it was not necessary to be verbal. I could sense his love for me and that was more than enough. Sameer knew everything about me, right from the time I use to wake up, till the time I retired to bed again. He was aware of my day's schedule, my plans for the weekend, till the extent that he knew by friend's birthdates by heart.

'Tomorrow is Sophia's birthday, don't forget,' he said one day.

That time I realised that my life has become so focussed on Sameer, that besides him I tend to forget about everything and everyone else.

'You forget means you don't care,' this was what my class teacher in standard 5 used to say. It was not entirely true, but part of it was correct. Recently I had neglected my friends a lot. I used to skip going to the gatherings, if they call I did not bother to call them back, it had been a long time that I went to see Nikhil's football match and since a long time I did not go to Maria's house for a dinner or lunch. The case was also reverse. I no longer invited them home, while in the past we used to gather at my place every weekend. I did not make movie or dinner plans, where as in the past I used to be the one to always bring up something or another. It was actually all my fault. While one side I was taking counselling sittings to come close to my parents, at the same time, on another side was drifting far away from my friends. This was not at all moving in a positive direction and I had to think about this seriously.

Not only this, even my parents at home behaved a little differently. Actually once while Sameer and I were sitting in a lounge, I thought I had seen my neighbour there. But then I did not pay much attention. May be she must have told my mom about it. As such my parents trusted me a lot. They would only feel sad that their own daughter was not telling them; rather they were getting to know things from the outsiders.

'Stick to your lectures,' dad had again used those indirect expressions and mom also gave me those looks at the dining table, as if she wanted to give me a hint that she knows something. But I did not want to tell them about Sameer. It was still not the right time. I was too very young for it and still things weren't settled between us. So I continued to behave the same. But there was a remarkable change in me, after my sittings with Dr. Monica. Whatever she used to suggest and asked me to do, I applied that at home, and in course of time I realised that things had started becoming easy. This was all due to the healing tonic, love. It was not that I used to rush home after college and tell my parents, 'Oh, I love you both', but I used to put the same thing in different ways.

One day when I was dressing up for college, mom was in the kitchen, boiling vegetables. I went to her and asked her to choose my top.

'What do you think will look good mom, the yellow one or the white?'

She had a very surprised look on her face but I could see she liked it. Like this I had started involving her in my everyday things and she was more than pleased about it. I was not doing it, because Dr. Monica had assigned me the task, I was doing it because I really liked her suggestions. I admired the way she cared for me.

With dad also, situations turned better. He had a habit of taking tea after returning from office. His routine habit was to go in the kitchen, set up the stove and by the time the tea used to get ready, he used to get fresh. One day however, when he got back home, I was sitting in the living room, watching television.

'I want to drink tea, should I make for you too?' I asked him.

Dad always reacted differently. Whenever he liked something, or he was surprised, he would answer in a yes or no.

'Make three cups then', mom had said.

It was after ages that the three of us were having the evening tea together. This became a routine for us then. Actually tea was just a support, while having it, I noticed that three of us, did healthy discussions, mom spoke about her patients and dad told us about his clients. I was the audience there, but I liked listening to them. After a long time, I was not listening from my ears; I was listening from my heart.

It was my parent's wedding anniversary. Every year, we used to go to a boring dinner, as usual order a Punjabi platter, eat, and watch other families in the surrounding table and drive back home. This year however I did not want the sequence to repeat. That year, I had prepared a handmade *khadi* card for them. In the card I wrote everything what I wanted to tell them but was not able to do orally. Some things are better written than spoken and at least for people like me, writing was one of the best options to go with. That year instead of going out, I suggested mom to cook dad's favourite dishes at home. I had helped her out and before dad came home from office, we had already set everything. We had arranged the food, for the three of us on the terrace. Setting up a small table and three chairs was not a difficult task. Dad had never been so pleased in his life when he saw all of it and that it was my idea amazed him more. That night we all ate in peace, but there was no more silence at the dinner table. Dad was recalling incidents about his past, the ones when they were caught watching a film in the cinema during their college time and the ones where dad had a severe thrashing from my grandmother, when he had completely forgotten their 2nd anniversary. It was fun to listen to those incidents, before this I did not know that my parents had such a colourful side too. After the dinner, I prepared three mugs of cold coffee, carried one with myself and retired in my den, while I allowed mom and dad to laugh on the sweet happy memories of their past.

Chapter 13

Just a week after the start of summer vacation, Sameer was leaving for Dubai for some official work. He had laid hands on a big project and if it worked out, it would be like his forever dream coming true. He was looking forward to this with a lot of excitement .I too was happy about it but at the same time I did not want him to go.

Since the time we met, none of us had travelled and now almost after three months, this was the first time I had to stay away from him. However, one major problem was, even he wasn't sure how as to how many days it could take. It all depended on the work there. There was a pure possibility of his staying for more than week, a fortnight or perhaps even a month. Nevertheless, one thing was certain, I had to talk to him and tell him what all I thought of in my mind.

Two days before his flight, Sameer and I met early for breakfast. We had decided to spend the whole day together, from morning to late evening. It was actually my idea because I wanted to spend as much time as possible with him before he took off.

To my surprise, he did not eat the breakfast at all.

'Not eating because of our separation?' I teased him.

He forced me a smile and said nothing.

After the breakfast, he took me to one of his sites, where he himself booked a house. The house was yet not ready but we saw it from within anyway. It was an apartment on the ground floor and the primary worked showed a possibility of a backyard with a personal garden space. It was exactly the kind of house which I ever dreamed of. My spirits were raised looking at it.

'I plan to stay here, once it is done.'

'It's lovely.'

'Just like you,' he added.

He pulled me very close to himself and we inaugurated the house-warming ceremony with a deep long lip-lock and I felt wonderful. Each time I kissed him, I felt great. It was like I used to get more charged up and since he was going; I needed a heavy dose to keep me going for the days ahead.

For lunch I insisted to go to a quiet place. We chose a place on the highway and Sameer was silent for the most of the time, as if something else was on his mind.

'Do you want to tell me anything?' I asked

'No, do you feel so?'

'Sort of.'

He was to leave day after the next, and I was feeling as if time was slipping away from my hands, my eyes remained moist during the entire lunch and my emotional mind had completely shadowed my practical senses.

'I don't know but I feel as if, as if I am losing you.'

'Don't be silly. I am not going forever. I will be back before you even realise it.'

The rest of the afternoon we shopped around for shirts, trousers, toiletries and all those things which he required to take along. We picked up a couple of formal shirts and I did not know why he was so inclined upon choosing the orange shades. He bought one shirt of my choice too and when he tried it, in my estimation he never looked so handsome before. It was almost the supper time, until we finished the shopping fiesta and came out of the mall. Hunger had taken its toll and we dined at one of the most exotic restaurants of the city.

After the dinner we went on the bridge. The shimmering water made hundreds of ripples just like the thoughts in my mind. Far away the light of the city felt like tiny little lamps brightening the dark sky. We were standing next to each other, just an inch apart; the same way like we were standing the first time in the café. It was I who broke the silence.

'It is time Sameer that I tell you something about myself.'

I told him everything right from the start. He listened carefully about my parents who adopted me, how much they loved me and how I felt about them. I told him incidents of my childhood when my mom had sleepless nights just because I had chicken pox and my dad missed his movie every weekend only to take me to the zoo. I explained to him what all I always and ever felt and about my talks with Dr. Monica and when I had finished it was for the first time I cried before him.

I expected him to hold me close, rather take me in his arms after I was done. But he did neither of that and simply nodded and continued the conversation.

'I understand everything but why this social work thing?' he asked.

'As I said I want to do something for children but I don't want any monitory benefits from it. Sameer, this society has given me a lot, a name, an identity, good parents, reliable friends and a lot more than I could ever imagine. I think I own a lot to this society and I need to serve it.'

'I can understand Tamanna. You are a special girl and your parents love you a lot.'

I looked at him, right in his eyes and asked him, 'and what about you?'

I knew that whatever his answer would be, positive or negative, it would make a world lot of difference to me.

He held both my hands in his, and spoke very gently but very firmly, 'I love you Miss Tamanna Habib.'

'I love you too, Sameer.'

I hugged him as tight as possible and for a long time cried my heart out. It was a feeling which I had never experienced before; the way I felt that time, was something so special that I would never forget.

He gifted me a long silver chain with a heart pendant. The pendant had a matt and copper shade with a blue stone embedded in between. It was lovely. He made me wear it in the car before he dropped me home. I asked him to drive slowly because I did not want the house to come soon. I kissed him gently on the lips before leaving.

'I will miss you Sameer.'

'I will miss you, too. Take good care of yourself.'

'Shall I wait for your call?'

'That's the first thing I'll do once I reach there.'

'Bye…take care.'

That night it was long before slumber bound me. Before closing my eyes I thought only and only about Sameer. It was lovely, the way he spoke his feeling out to me on the bridge. I tried evaluating, why he did not show any reaction when I told him about the adoption. Then I thought that may be some people are not that expressive. They do care, but they cannot show it out. They are introverts when it comes to reveal one's feelings and often such people are thought to be arrogant or the ones carrying an attitude. May be Sameer was one of those kinds for whom showing out his feelings was a little difficult. When I closed my eyes, I was absolutely sure about one thing, I knew Sameer loved me and I knew I loved him too. What I did not know was that it was for the last time that I saw him like that.

PART II

Chapter1

'You are the best thing that has ever happened to me,' Ryan had said, holding me close.

We were sleeping in each other's arms for the past two hours and none of us felt like getting up and continuing the day. We could cuddle under the sheets for hours together and never had enough of it. Finally I got up, against my wishes and heading towards the kitchen, I turned around and asked him,

'Would you like some coffee?'

'I prefer tea,' he said and we blushed at each other.

Ryan was a final year BSc student pursuing from the same college where I studied. I had not seen or met him until eight months ago, though I had heard his name several times when my classmates or other collegians mentioned the core committee. Ryan was the head of the core committee and it was a month prior to the college annual culfest that we had met. The core group had organised a meeting for the members who were to perform in the college drama. Since I was one of the participants, I was also present in the meeting.

Although I was terrible at acting, I did play some roles well. This drama was about a family of four, who gets separated during the 2000 earthquake. The parents lose their two kids, who are now staying in a rehabilitation camp. The drama was structured on the girl who put's the world's efforts to unite the family. The girl was the main character in the drama, and her role was assigned to me.

'Do I look like someone who has just returned from a rehabilitation camp?' I had asked my drama colleagues.

Ryan addressed the core members and giving us a detailed list of scheduled rehearsals, instructed all other things that were to take into consideration. He was an ordinary looking guy, nothing special about him and I was least bothered to even remember his face. We practised for almost one month putting our hearts and souls into it but just two days prior to the drama, things became a little deformed.

I rushed into the cabin where he sat, didn't even bother to' greet him or anything and said in an anger that made my cheeks go red.

'You can't do this,' I had said.

'Do what?'

'You just can't change my dialogues the last minute. I can't mug them up and act them out in so short a span.'

'Yes you can,' he had adamantly replied and left the room. I had felt as if the door had been slammed on my face.

Our drama turned out to be an extraordinary one. It was only that my eyes were puffed up and had dark circles around them due to lack of two nights sleep. It only made look like some sort of malnourished.

He had come to me after the drama and had said, 'You were simply amazing. If you don't mind can I have an honour to have coffee with an actor?'

I was damn pissed off due to this whole thing and if there was one person's whose head I wanted to bang, it was Ryan's, but the way he asked me, it was simple impossible to resist.

For a while, I had just looked at him and had said, 'I prefer tea.'

We had both smiled and this is how it had started.

We can never know God's plans. Our lives are so pre-defined, much before we know. I wonder how destiny unites and separates people. Sometimes even the things gone ugly in the initial stages, turns out to be lovely in the end.

My anger towards him had long ago evaporated, for Ryan was an easy friend to make. He was easy going, lively and fun to be with and I was amazed thinking how easily I got acquainted with him. Ryan's parents both were dentists and when he had told me that, the first thing I did was noticed his teeth. It was not that I wanted to observe his teeth but my eyes just automatically felt there. He had even, white teeth, nothing special about them but when he laughed, it added an extra charm to his face. His face was not that photogenic but in a way it was appealing. The calmness of it attracted people towards him.

Ryan was a man of the world, a true social animal by all means. Whenever I saw him, he was surrounded by a group of people, sometimes it seemed that he was engrossed in listening what others were telling him and at times he had a circle of crowd around him and he was speaking to them as if being some kind of a preacher.

Once when we were sitting in the cinema theatre, for the movie which I wanted to watch so very desperately, and when it was about to start, Ryan was called by one of his friend who was on the verge of his break up with his girlfriend. He rushed to offer his condolences, unaware of the fact that if he continued to behave in this manner, very soon his friends will revert to console him for his breakup.

Yet another time, when we were under the sheets, Ryan received a call from his classmate's brother, asking for some advice on career options. He said he needed to fill in some application form and it was urgent. Ryan has just grabbed his clothes, didn't even bother to comb his hair or look himself in the mirror and rushed to his place, only to select a university for him and I like an idiot was alone under the covers waiting for him to return.

'Oh God, look at me also sometime, I am your girlfriend', I got annoyed, and as a matter of fact had lost my cool and had yelled at him.

From that day he made it a point to keep people at a bay. He started using all possible shortcuts in the college premises where minimum people would dash him. He minimised his social circles and stopped giving his contacts to the freshers and most importantly he simple switched off his phone whenever we made love.

'You don't need to go to this extent, Ryan', I had told him.

'I am not doing it for you Tamanna, I am doing it for myself. I want to spend more and more time with you.'

Like English is a funny language, love is a hilarious obsession. It makes people do weird things which they have never thought even in their wildest dreams. People happen to propose their loved ones, when they are out for dinner or when something exclusive is planned, but in my case, I wasn't proposed rather asked to confess. It was exactly four months after we had met that Ryan and I were walking at a nearby stall to eat corn. The monsoons had set in and it had rained right from the dusk. Everything around was fresh, green and lively, it was as if romance was in the air. There were puddles of water everywhere. After College we had kept our bags and umbrellas in the car itself and folded our denims till our knees and had walked for almost two kilometres to eat corn. I was busy nibbling the corn when all of a sudden he had looked at me and had said,

'Tamanna, do you love me?' I had looked at him quizzically.

'Oh come on! I can see it in your eyes. So just say it,' he said.

When I had answered in an affirmative he had dumped his corn aside and had lifted me high and for a second even I wasn't bothered about the audience glancing our way. When we got back home, we were completely drenched from head to toe and though my cold was okay in a day, Ryan carried a red nose, watery eyes and sneezing senses for almost a week.

Like this we had tried several other things and it was as if Ryan was my best friend. In his presence I never felt lonely or never required anyone else.

Chapter 2

Not that Ryan was a professional photographer, but he clicked exceptionally well. He had taken a short term photography course during the mid-summer vacation and he was very fond of doing outdoor photography. In fact he had purchased a professional camera, along with its stand and all, bit by bit, gathering money, whatever he saved due to cost cutting. Unlike me, Ryan was a more stable person when it came to hobbies and interests. I was a live example of Jack of all trades and master of none. As a child and even as a teenager, I had tried all possible things like Karate, skating, calligraphy, ceramic and canvas painting, learning guitar among many others. I had indeed wasted a lot of my parent's money, during every summer breaks, than used to leave things half way and after a fortnight, get some other crazy thought and pursued that. But Ryan as I said was much more stable. Photography was his only hobby and interest. His room had a big collection of books on photography, one that taught you everything about the field, and his soft board was pasted with several different photographs, one on river side, another of an ocean, yet another of some butterfly and so on. He used to get his photographs framed and gifted to people and all of them were as lovely as one could imagine. It was actually difficult to say which one was the best.

'You should really take this business seriously', I had told him, when he had gifted me one of his most favourite photograph on Valentine's Day. It was a picture, clicked on a sea-shore, during sunset in which a couple held hands, and was walking on the beach.

'I want us to stay like this forever,' he had said.

One evening we had gone to the Gandhi Ashram. We used to often go there and sit on the river banks. It was a quiet place and settling sun was a beautiful scene to behold. If people wanted to hunt me in cinema halls, shopping malls and cafes, I would mention they would have a tuff time. I wasn't a person amidst the crowd. I liked quiet places, away from the world.

'Why don't you go and stay in a jungle,' Ryan had teased me when I use to give me options like Gandhi Ashram, Thol Lake and other such aloof places. But then I used to show him the greed of photography and he would simply go with the plan.

That evening when he was taking pictures, I had told him about my parents and that I was seeing a clinical psychologist. I knew he would be a little shocked and would be okay after few minutes, and so it happened. I always knew how Ryan would act in a particular situation, or what will his expressions be when he was disturbed or confused. We sat for a long time there that evening and talked a lot on this topic. It was after all important for him to know.

My parents tried a lot for a child of their own but somehow it just didn't happen. After several tests and treatments, the doctors told them that though my mother was totally okay, my dad was the one who required the medication. His treatment continued for almost three years, after which it was declared that nothing can be worked out. By that time, everyone in my parent's friends circle had one or two kids and though my mom never expressed her sorrow, for the fear how dad would feel, she always aspired for a child. It was long after my grandparents had suggested adopting a child and my parents started consulting the orphanage.

'I don't know Ryan, if they hadn't adopted me, where I would be now, with whom and in which condition.'

'You don't need to think much, the present is more important. Don't think of things which never happened.'

'I don't know how your parents will take this,' I told him.

'Leave that to me, don't strain yourself.'

Chapter 3

My parents had easily accepted Ryan and as far as his parents were concerned they liked me since the time they saw the drama on the CD. Ryan knew everything about my parenthood right from the start. With him there were never any secrets. I didn't find it difficult to tell him about it all for I knew he would understand and when I had told him all, he had held me in his arms for a long time and kissed me gently on the forehead.

A week after he proposed me, Ryan had come home to meet my parents. I told him to act as if finding the house was a little difficult for him, for I didn't wanted to take any chances. I didn't wanted my parents to sense anything and have any doubts. Officially Ryan was coming home for the first time, unofficially the visits were several. He seemed to be a little nervous confronting my dad but I knew that all would go well, for Ryan had one of the finest hearts in the world.

The visit turned out to be better than I had expected. My mom liked him a lot and my dad spend almost two hours with him after dinner, talking about his old days until I kept on giving missed calls to Ryan to make him get up and come to me.

Dr. Monica's sittings had helped me a lot. I went to her for almost a year. She counselled me and gave me more confidence. In one of the session's she wanted to meet my parents. When I had told them that I was seeing a psychologist because my adoption bothered me they seemed to be a little hurt. For a few days there was no conversation between us, unless required. Nor that they were angry or anything but just a little more concerned. They came for the same anyway.

The doctor called us each one of us simultaneously. I was the first she talked with. I told her not to mention anything that would hurt either of them. I had already hurt them much. She knew that more than me and after talking with me for a while called my dad inside.

I yet don't know what conversation they had inside; according to the rules it is not to be disclosed. But after sometime when my dad walked out he seemed to be much more relaxed. But the main thing was still to come. The most difficult person to deal with was my mom. My mother was a very sensitive person. She worked, talked, acted and behaved purely through her emotional guidance system. When a person is more sensitive and emotional, more than what is required, it is sometimes dangerous. Such people tend to cry very fast, get angry very soon and may over react even in normal situations for their mind is not at all ready to accept the particular world.

Mom's session continued for an entire hour. Dad and I were sitting in the reception next to each other but hardly conversed. I could see from the corner of my eye that he wanted to avoid any talks and so I too didn't press. I kept texting Ryan, updating him with every second's details while dad got engrossed in a boring business magazine which he often read.

After an hour when dad and I went inside, I knew what to expect. Mom had been crying since the time she had gone inside. But everything that day was sorted out. My parents accepted my retirement plans from studies after I finished college. They were not very happy about it but they wanted me to be happy. According to them that was one of the most important things. Mom and dad accepted the NGO proposal also which I had put forward. To dad especially this had come as a shock. Looking at the kind of person I was, extravagant expenses, and mischievous behaviour dad could imagine me to adopt any other profession except social service. But after a few days he too became normal.

That night my mom came to my room and made me sleep in her lap.

'You were a year old Tamanna, when you came home. Like this only you slept in my arms for most of the night. I had caressed you all night, looked at you and loved you since the moment I held you in my arms. I never thought even for a second that you are not the product of my own womb. That night I saw certain dreams not only for you but also for myself. And from that time I started seeing the world from your eyes. I didn't see you as a model or a doctor or somebody, I wanted to leave that option to you, but I was determined about one thing. I wanted you to be a good person. I wanted you to be a person that would make us feel proud one day. Today is one of the happiest days of my life. You have proved yourself to be one of the best daughters in this world. You are a very good person Tamanna who cares about her parents and her friend. I am proud of you and I am sure your father also feels the same.'

'I love you, mom.'

'I love you too.'

I don't know when mom left my room for I had slept very peacefully that night. All my burdens were released. All my tensions were gone and the next day when I woke up things were back to normal again. We were after many days chirping and laughing just like the same way they show in typical family movies in the end.

Dr. Monica also liked Ryan a lot. She was pleased to meet him. Not that she had anything to tell him precisely but it was the last time I was going to meet her so I dragged Ryan along. I had made a bookmark for her and she was delighted as usual when she met me.

'So this is Ryan? Huh! Heard about you a lot,' she had said.

'I hope all positive,' Ryan had said.

'Absolutely!'

There was nothing much left to talk and so our visit was short and more casual this time. Dr. Monica wished me luck for all my future endeavours and told me to always keep a positive outlook towards life. Ryan and I had left her clinic in a glee.

Chapter 4

I had gone to Ryan's house for dinner that evening. His parents were lovable people. Ryan's parents had a love marriage and it was a plus point for us. I was a bit hesitant and I admit I was scared when I had to face his parents. I knew they liked me, they had no problem at all with mine and Ryan's relation but still I meeting someone face to face, officially is a big thing. When I kept on insisting Ryan to come and meet my parents, I thought it was no big deal, but when the same thing applied to me, I understood that one needs to have real guts.

Ryan had a beautiful house, one with long glass windows and an excellent taste of colour combinations. The house had been recently furnished and with the walls filled with Ryan's photographs, the house looked livelier.

'Who's the architect?' I asked.

Actually this was always my first question whenever I stepped into a good house, or even at a new restaurants or any other elegant place. I used to not do this before but at least since past one and half years, I had started doing this.

The meeting turned out to be better than I had expected. Instead of asking how my parents were doing and how was college going, Ryan's parents asked me about my future NGO projects.

'I really appreciate the work you're planning to do. The country needs such inputs,' Ryan's father had said. Not only this, his mom also gave me two-three good references of the people whom she thought would be interested in such social service work. Like Ryan his parents were also totally unexpected.

Later after dinner, Ryan and I sat on his terrace and I cried and cried because I did not want him to leave me alone and go.

Two weeks later Ryan left for Australia to pursue his further studies. He was keen upon getting master degrees and besides everything he took his career very seriously. Although he had given me numerous gifts starting from silver rings and chains to soft toys and cards. This time however he gifted me a diary.

'Call this your wish diary,' he had told me.

'I want you to write all that you wish to do once I am back and we are married. Assemble your thoughts in this and we will implement them once we are at a threshold of our new life.'

Ryan was never predictable. He used to surprise me most of the times and this was one of the reasons I kept falling in love with him over and over again.

I went to see him off at the airport. He had kissed me and spoken three loveable words.

'I love you.'

'I love you too, Ryan. I love you a lot. Please take care of yourself and come back soon.'

When he moved away from me, he kept walking until he reached the check-in counter. He had turned and looked at me. I smiled at him and thought that unlike before I am sure I'll see him again very soon.

Chapter 5

'This is not possible.'

'Yes it is. It is true. Sameer and I have been married for two and half years now,' Shalini said.

Shalini Raheja was Sameer Raheja's wife. So Sameer had been married even before we were seeing each other. For a moment it had all appeared to me as a joke but when Shalini showed me their wedding snaps all my doubts had vanished. This news came to me as a sudden unexpected blow.

When Sameer had left for Dubai and college had been closed for summer vacations. I had nothing much to do. I used to get up late so that I had to think less about him during the day. I did all the household chores so that I kept myself occupied and didn't miss him much and rest of my time I spent with my friends having chilled lemonades to beat the heat or laughing on silly jokes and thinking about funny professors or cursing the education system.

That afternoon I was chilling at Maria's place giggling on all the girly talks which to anyone else would appear totally senseless. It was that time when my cell phone rang loudly and I wasn't at all aware that that particular call could shift my entire world.

The call was from Sameer's mother and she insisted to see me that very day. There was urgency in her voice and I could sense that and a part of me sensed that there was something very wrong somewhere.

That evening I went to Sameer's residence and when I rang the doorbell a young lady had opened the door. That young lady was none other than Shalini Raheja. Sameer's house was exactly the same that he had often described. The living room was painted in crème and the while entering from the main door was a small fish pond. There were two gold fish in it, the way Sameer used to say. The right side of the living room had a criss-cross open cabinet, which contained books on various topics like design, construction, architecture and trends. Towards the left was the seating arrangement where I was sitting. I had never seen such a beautiful house before, everything right from the chandeliers, artefacts, wall pieces and centre and corner tables, all were as if made on demand. Needless to mention, Sameer had an exceptionally classy and chic taste.

An hour later when Shalini told me everything, and after I saw the snaps, things started falling into pieces. The person who had called me up earlier was not Sameer's mother but it was Shalini, his wife who had pretended to be his mom.

'I had my doubt since many days, but I was waiting for the right time,' Shalini said. It was then clear to me that Shalini might be sneaking after Sameer for many days. She must have jotted my number from his cell phone and would know much about Sameer and me, than I had anticipated. But I did not ask her whether she had ever followed Sameer when he came to meet me or whether anyone from outside sources told her about our affair. One thing was sure, Shalini was smart enough to track us down, and she had hit the moment at the spurt of the time. Where as one side I was angry on Sameer and wanted to support Shalini, at the same time, I was a bit hesitant as to how much to open my tongue and disclose the affair. It was that most of the time Shalini did the talking and I kept quiet.

I know understood why Sameer had kept only certain hours for calling and texting, why was he confused when I first asked him about his family on our first meeting, why at times he used to behave differently.

'I have a family,' he had said. I know understood what he meant by the word family.

Shalini's attitude towards me was neutral for she knew that had I known that Sameer was already settled I would never set a relationship with him.

As soon as I had heard about his being married, I had started crying. My eyes were overflowing with tears and I felt claustrophobic. I left his house as soon as Shalini had finished her part of the story and when I was leaving Shalini asked me that I should never meet her husband again.

Before leaving I had asked Shalini one question, 'What is your favourite colour Shalini?'

'Orange, why?'

'Nothing.'

I had cried and trembled all the way home and I had so many thoughts about Sameer, about Shalini, about our relationship and about their relationship and about everything and when I reached home I had to act as if everything was okay, as If I had just returned home from Maria's place. That evening I went to my room after eating only a morsel of food and I simply told my parents that I was very tired and that I wanted to sleep. When I checked the Facebook profile clearly, by entering two three different combinations, adding Sameer's surname and middle name, I came to know that he actually had two different accounts.

That night I had thoughts all over again and still I wasn't able to believe what all Shalini had mentioned about their marriage. I had to tell myself hundred times that Sameer was a married man, he had a wife and the thought that Sameer was somebody's husband almost killed me.

That night I felt victimised. I felt cheated. I wanted to hate him for all this and part of me hated him but I had several questions to ask him. He just couldn't play with me or my emotions like this. He didn't had that right to it with me or with anyone else. I wanted all my answers. If I told Sameer over the phone or e-mailed him regarding this, situation would slip entirely from my hands. So I decided to behave normally with him whenever he called from Dubai. It was pretty difficult to pretend especially when you know that someone so close to you has ditched you. Although Shalini had asked me not to see Sameer anymore, I was determined to meet him once and confront him for it was just not about Shalini and Sameer, it was equally about Sameer and myself.

Chapter 6

Shalini and Sameer were like soul mates. They knew each other since childhood. They had played together, fought with each other, went to the same school, and their parents were neighbours ever since Sameer's dad shifted here from Delhi. Shalini's brother, Vivek, was Sameer's best friend and since Vivek and Sameer grew up together, Shalini was very much a part of Sameer's upbringing. With the passage of time, they both got so used to each other, that it was impossible for them to except someone else in their lives, and ever since Sameer understood what love was, there was only one name in his mind,SHALINI.

The only time, they got separated when Sameer went to study architecture and Shalini's father bought a new house and the family re-located. But still the strings of attachment never got ruptured and they continued the affair the way it was. There was no scope of proposing each other or going into any formality, for not only Sameer and Shalini were sure about their wedding but even their families equally liked the pair and they very soon got engaged when Sameer was in his last semester.

As a couple, Shalini and Sameer were very compatible. They had a great bonding, amazing chemistry between them. They used to fight on petty things and never wanted to see each other's faces but then again the next day, they were spotted together. Sameer was very possessive about her; he never used to let her wear short skirts or revealing necks, except when he was with her.

On Shalini's twentieth birthday, Sameer had given her exactly twenty red roses. On the following Valentine's Day, he had made Shalini wear a diamond ring, which Shalini still wore till date. Not only this, before their wedding, Sameer had gifted Shalini and her friends an exclusive holiday package to Goa and on their wedding night, Sameer had gifted Shalini, the house in which they were living at present.

One day, Shalini wanted to go for a movie and when they reached the theatre, the show was houseful. Sameer had gone to extremes, requested two people, who had already bought the tickets to give it to him and in turn he had bought them two tickets in an ebony lounge for the next day. It had cost him double the actual price of the movie, but it was as if Shalini's wish was his command. In the same way, a month after their wedding, Shalini wanted to eat a pizza, somewhere around 2 a.m. Sameer had searched the whole city, called couple of his friends and got to know where he would find someone who would prepare a pizza so late. He had specially requested the pizza and by the time he came back it was 4 a.m. in the morning. People say that love is blind and at that time Sameer was an ideal example to prove this phrase.

For their honeymoon, Sameer had taken Shalini to South Africa. There they had explored the places, walked over the towns, made love under the open moon, had midnight coffees, late night drinks and did all those possible things which a girl could ever desire for her honeymoon. I knew that Sameer was romantic, but he was so romantic, I did not know.

Sameer had done everything to make Shalini feel happy. He used to go overboard and do extreme things for her. I did not know why Shalini narrated me all these incidences, but it appeared as if she wanted someone to listen to her.

'Things change after marriage,' she said. And I had just kept quiet.

Shalini was the person who liked luxury, who loved getting up late, who preferred a bed tea, instead stirring it up herself. She preferred sitting at home and watching television, when it was pouring outside, or go to sleep when she got holidays. But Sameer was altogether different. He liked adventure, he liked to walk under the rain, he liked the rays of the sun touching his skin, he preferred to roam late night on the highways, or go for hiking camps whenever he got some free time.

'Sameer doesn't love me anymore. He wants someone fresh now. He considers me outdated. I am no longer the one about whom he was crazy.'

Hearing about Shalini and Sameer's love history pricked me. I did not want to hear it but I did not even have any option. I was in no position to console Shalini, because what all she said was already hard for me to digest. What I thought that even though Shalini and Sameer were best of friends, they were not perfect to be each other's life partners. I had thoughts which I never wanted to think. I imagined their honeymoon, I visualised their daily living, I thought about their childhood and the time when Shalini was Sameer's everything. How I suddenly came into Sameer's life, changed the entire scenario. This was making things difficult and it was all Sameer's fault. He knew this phase would come, where all three of us will have to face pain, yet he went on.

Chapter 7

There was only one thing on my priority list, meeting Sameer as soon as possible but I had no other option than to wait. Yet that wait had almost killed me. It was as if my life had come to a standstill, it had completely stopped moving. I had completed sunk into a remotest depression state. I was aloof from my friends and family and it was that time when I started writing a diary and penned down everything from the time I met Sameer till the moment what I felt in the present. It was as if I wanted to tell all this to someone but I did not want anyone to feel sorry for me, or console me or fill my mind with advices. I wanted someone to just listen to me and I thought that spilling the beans in the diary would be the best thing to do. I would go for long walks often early in the morning or late evenings and would think all the time about only one person. My biological clock was disturbed and there was nothing like a normal routine for me. I woke up at odd times, sometimes in the middle of night and at times I use to sleep almost at dusk. I would go on the bridge and observe the water and I would not even realise that I was crying. I would think about the happy times I spent with Sameer and thinking how badly this is going to end, made my heart ache.

I remember one day we had gone to the park for a walk. It was a cold January morning, just a few days after we had first met. I had worn a red t-shirt and I was freezing because the chilled breeze gave me goose bumps all over. At the time Sameer had given me his jacket, and I had felt very cosy in it. Later after the walk when I returned his jacket he had told me,

'I am not going to wash this till the time I don't really have to.'

'Why, anything special?'

'It now carries your smell and that's more than enough for me,' he had said.

Just I had good memories with him, I also had bad memories when we fought, when I cried all night and when we didn't talk to each other for days. But I never wanted to recall those memories. However, time and situation had opened the gates of endless memories flooding my mind that I would literally get tired thinking about it all. At times I used to decide that now onwards I am going to be strong, I will be moving ahead and that I'll stop thinking and loving Sameer but then again my thoughts kept on diverting in that direction how much ever I tried. It was as if my mind was trapped in some sort of a cob web.

Love is beautiful but when something like this happens it takes a lot of strength to bear it. Loneliness literally killed me and at that time I felt that only two persons understood me more than anyone else. One was Maria and another was Nikhil. They both knew Sameer very well and they both like him, until I disclosed this fact to them. Maria had just kept quiet and Nikhil was more than furious. But it was because of them that I was able to bear what came my way. They listened to me, whatever I muttered with patience and never asked me to shut up. Although Nikhil didn't want me to weep, he said that Sameer was not worth my tears, Maria wanted me to cry and finish it once and for all. They stayed closed to me, called me up now and then, made plans to take me out and dropped at my place whenever they found time.

'Get ready, I am coming to pick you,' Maria said.

'Where are we going?' I was frustrated. I didn't wanted to go anywhere.

'You'll love it,' she said.

Twenty minutes later we were at the orphanage. Maria knew the head there and she had also taken a prior appointment. The orphanage needed some volunteers who would visit the children once a week and conduct special sessions and since Maria knew what I wanted to do in my future she thought this to be the best way to begin my career. It was a small community centre, painted in white with a small garden and a little of a play area. I immediately accepted the proposal and made plans for the coming class. I was excited about the whole thing.

'After ages I see you smiling.'

'Thanks Maria. You are a great friend.'

I conducted sessions with the children. They were between the age group of 4-14 years and the kids were lovely. I used to teach them different things. One day I taught them Origami, in another session I taught them how to make candles and in one session I took them to the garden and taught the names of different plants and flowers.

Doing this made me felt good. It was not that I was not thinking about Sameer, but this activity relaxed me and the pain became more bearable. One day as I was walking back home from the orphanage after my session, my cell phone rang.

'Hello.'

'Hey, I am back. I didn't tell you because I wanted to give you a surprise.'

'Shall we meet for dinner tonight?'

I could bet millions that I never wanted to meet Sameer so desperately before.

Chapter 8

Ryan knew everything about Sameer. I had told him about it in the initial stages of our relationship. Though I hadn't told him all the details that what had happened between us, I had told him everything that he was required to know. I didn't want someone else from outside to come and tell him. I had just told him in the end that Sameer was different guy, our frequency didn't match and we had several differences and so we mutually broke up. This is again one good lie. Sometimes it is best not to mention everything. The less your present knows about your past, the better it is. This avoids misunderstandings and one can live happily with the present.

I never compared Sameer and Ryan. Both were different personalities, different individuals altogether. While Sameer had that looks that left girls staring him in awe, Ryan was ordinary looking. Sameer used to do things according to his logical brain, Ryan on the other hand was more on a creative side. Sameer liked to keep to himself, while Ryan enjoyed people hovering around him. But there was something common between the two. They both loved me.

While having dinner with Sameer on the night he returned, I kept my cool. We only talked about his trip, about his work there and for most of the part it was he who was doing the speaking and I was simply nodding my head.

'You look thin, Tamanna,' he said, 'You are not eating?'

I had kept quiet that time too and he told me how much he remembered me there when he saw wonderful things there, how much he missed me every moment of everyday. After the dinner we decided to go for a stroll and that is where I told him in a firm but soft voice.

'I met your wife, Shalini.'

I told him that I went to his house and had come to know that he was married. I also told him how Shalini had called me up, faking to be his mother. I was shouting at him while mentioning all this and my words were full of wrath.

'You cheat, you used me. You did time pass with me and now do you care to explain'? I told him with anger dripping from my every breath.

Although Sameer was shocked listening to whatever I said, he didn't get angry. He didn't know from where Shalini got my number, probably from his cell.

'Tamanna, I love my wife.'

These words came to me as a bitter realty which tore my heart. But he continued.

'At the same time I love you too. I accept the fact that I didn't tell you that I was married but I never intended to use you in anyway. I wanted to tell you right from the start of our relationship but I never had the guts. I didn't have that much courage. I wanted to tell you when I returned from my trip, but before I could get a chance, you came to know already. Trust me, I didn't want you to know all this in such a bad way.'

When he spoke there were tears of concern in his eyes, but he continued.

'I genuinely like you girl and when I started spending time with you, I realised how much I loved your company. You are a different girl Tamanna. You are that bubbly girl, which made my day. Whenever I went to office and thought about you, I would start thinking what shade of nail paint you must be applying today, whether you must have matched your earring with the dress or not. I used to do things with you that I never used to do with anyone else, not even my wife and other friends. It's not with every other person I watch the sunrise Tamanna, it's not with everyone I sit and discuss my view. You were one with whom my mind was compatible and this drew me more and more towards you. I didn't even realise when I fell in love with you. But I was afraid that if I told you, you would never get friendly with me and I'll never get a chance to come close to you. I know I was being selfish, hurting you in the process. Please forgive me.'

'You knew we had no future, then why did you even think of coming close to me?'

'Life is too short to love just one person Tamanna and life is too short to love everyone in only one way. I am not saying that I go and love everybody whom I get in touch with. But some people are special. They make a place in your heart even before you come to know and you are such a person. Believe me I have never come across anybody like you. I knew we had no future together, but I didn't wanted to lose your company, just thinking about the future. I was afraid to tell you that I loved you. I never wanted to say those words because I knew it would hurt you more but when I told you that I love you, it seemed as if this was what I always felt for you. It appeared right to me and I went with the waves rather than going against the tide.'

'So now what do you expect from me?'

'I don't expect anything from you and in the past also I never expected anything from you. I just wanted you to be happy. I just wanted you to do what makes you happy. And today also I wish the same for you. If you have anything to tell me than please say it out, I don't want you to carry that burden in your heart forever. I don't want you to ruin your life, have sleepless nights, waste your time and most importantly I don't want you to not fall in love again.'

'I am not going to meet you Sameer. I am not going to see you anymore. I liked you and loved you a lot. I still do. But I don't want to walk in a direction where there is no future. I don't want to create confusions. I don't want broken hearts and messy lives anymore.'

'I respect your thoughts.'

Sameer dropped me home that night and while driving back I knew this was finally over. When I was about to get down he kissed me one last time on my forehead.

'Take care of yourself, Tamanna. I will always love you.'

'Take care.'

With that he was gone. I waited at the gate watching the car till the time it vanished from my sight. That night while going to bed, I had no thoughts at all. I didn't even try to recall the day. My mind was absolutely vacant and I felt as if I was floating in space. I felt so light.

Chapter 9

About one thing I was damn sure, that I would never meet Sameer again. I would try to keep myself very busy. I would get indulge in any sports, or hobby or anything that would restrict me from thinking about him. But it was not that easy, as I had thought. Sameer's thoughts, memories were always on my mind. Even though I was watching television, I was thinking about it. Even while painting I was thinking about our relation. It was as if I wanted to go and bang my head with some wall and wanted to finish this once and for all.

One day, I was passing by Sameer's office. It was around 1 p.m. and I knew he would be free, since it was his lunch time. I wanted to go to a friend's place. Even though there were several routes to reach her place, I picked up the one that would bring Sameer's office in middle. I had texted him that afternoon.

'I am near your office.'

And in the next half hour we were together, sitting in Café Coffe Day, talking about anything crap that came into our heads.

'How's Nikhil?' he asked. Such were his questions because we both did not know what to talk.

'How is Shalini doing?' I asked.

'Fine'.

We did not stay for long; it was only for thirty minutes. But I felt good. Seeing him after so many days made me feel nice. I did not ask him whether he misses me or not, whether he thinks about me or not, we just kept our meeting very formal and restricted.

Actually I was going insane used to look around for Sameer in the crowd. Whenever I spotted some tall, fair boy, I thought it was him, even though I knew it wasn't him. I would look around for every white Optra in the city, from wherever I passed. I would type messages and then store them in the draft. I did not want to send him. I would go to the places where we had been together, I would watch the sunrise, the sunset and do every possible thing which he used to do. In a way doing all this, made me feel connected to him. I felt as if we were still into a relation. I had convinced my mind that Sameer was with me only.

A few days later, it was our six month anniversary and Sameer wanted to meet me that day. Perhaps if things wouldn't have gone wrong, we would have celebrated it with a lot of gale. But we met that evening anyways. Sameer and I had gone for a long drive and an ice-cream, but it was late at night. While returning home, I did not expect but he kept his hand on mine and together on the gear. It was a long time, since we had any physical relation and though it was slight a touch, it was inviting. We could not resist ourselves, rather I was not able to resist myself and we kissed.

But that night I gave all this second thought. I was going in a direction where there was no future possibility. My feeling for him cannot the fact that he was married. Today he is married, tomorrow he would have a child and all this was not healthy. I had to bring this to an end. I had to bring our relation to a stop and for that I met Sameer the following day for the last time.

It was a rainy day and dark clouds had filled the sky. My heart was also as gloomy as the day but I had to console myself, had to face the truth and so with a lot of guts I managed to speak it out.

'I cannot meet you anymore. You are already married. This is immoral.'

'Me being married cannot change our feelings, Tamanna.'

'Yes, but I don't want to walk on the path which does not fit into my moral scenario.'

We discussed a lot after this. Though I wanted to end all this, he did not want me to walk out of his life. Nevertheless I was firm. I cannot by any means take this any further. That was the last time I met Sameer Raheja, it was the June 3, and later that night, when I sat to write my diary, I noted the day and the date in black.

Chapter 10

It was the D day. It was my wedding day. I was on the threshold of my new life. I was on the verge of getting settled and this day was one of the most important days of my life. Just a few hours before my wedding I was seated in front of the dressing table in my room and was thinking about Sameer.

'Life is too short to love just one person,' he had said.

I didn't know whether that made sense to me or not but there was something. Sameer was the first person who added a different definition of love in my life. In his company, I understood how it is to love your partner. Today I love Ryan, I have absolutely no feelings for Sameer, but still I respect him, for if my heart is blooming with the colourful flowers of love for Ryan, it was Sameer who had planted its first seed.

Like all other girls who were on the verge of getting married, I also did all my preparations whole heartedly. I had gone to possibly all the shops in the city taking dress rehearsals before I picked up my wedding dress. I had taken care of my skin, my hair, my figure and everything to appear flawless on my wedding day. When the cards had come from the printing, I had personally written all the names on it, inviting people around. I had gone to my friends place to invite them and also posted to the ones who were far off. I had couriered one card at Sameer's office too, though I was sure he wouldn't come. Our relationship had ended on a very good note and so I thought that it was my duty to invite him. I had not thrown away his gifts. I still had that heart pendant and chain he had given me when he left for Dubai. Though I didn't wear it, I had kept it safely. It was a sweet remembrance of the happy times we spent together. I still respect Sameer and that feelings will never change till the time I am alive. But one thing I did before the wedding. I burnt the diary I had written before. At a stage where I was starting a new life, with the person whom I loved the most in this world, I didn't wanted to carry my past. I thought that it was the wisest thing to do. With each burning page, I wanted to kill all the emotions that I had or felt in the past for Sameer. But emotions are immortal, they never die, they can be just controlled.

When the make-up lady was dressing me for the ceremony, I told her,

'I want to appear the best today,' and I had also texted Ryan that I was nervous whether I will look beautiful or not.

'Of course you will. No one can look more beautiful than my wife on my wedding day,' he said.

Ryan's company was always motivating. Some people always carry positivity, a positive energy with them wherever they go and Ryan was one of them. When I went towards the hall, where the ceremonies were going to happen, with each step I took forward I was damn sure that I was marrying the right person. I had absolutely no doubts about it.

Epilogue

Last night I dreamed about my ex-boyfriend. He was dressed in a sky blue t-shirt and a beige pant and we were sitting somewhere on the steps having tea and discussing about some movie. I woke up with a jerk and my clock displayed that it was still midnight and my husband lay next to me on the bed. The next morning, my thoughts kept diverting towards him how much ever I ignored the thoughts. I did not wanted to recall my past love life, but it was as if his memories kept haunting me like a heavy tide and I was floating or rather being carried away with endless waves of memories dragging me towards the time when I was still eighteen, when my maturity was yet raw and when Sameer meant everything to me.

Ryan and I had been married for four years now. Like all other couples, we too often fought, made love and our life continued steadily till I came to know that I was expecting. All my dreams so far had come true. I wished to have loving parents, I had got that. If I had not gone to Dr. Monica Hiwale, I would never have analysed myself. Before that I was thinking that my parents stayed aloof from me because they don't love me, however the case was reverse. It was I who had made that mental block. But when I broke that barrier and tried to bridge the gap, I realised that I was the one who was keeping away from them. Sometimes we just jump to conclusions about a particular thing or person without allowing ourselves to use that thing or experiencing the person. Unless we do not try from our end, things will never change.

I was working as a volunteer with SP Child, a children's NGO for almost three years now. Most of my time was spent with children and I loved what I was doing. When I first got the news about becoming a mother, it was as if a different wing of love was added in my life. Just as we get use to things, in the same way we become habituated to people too. I can never imagine my life without Ryan.

My friends and cousins ask me often whether I do not ever get tired of Ryan, don't I get bored with him and has my love been the same since the time we knew each other. I laugh when they say so. I cannot explain them how it is to be in love. But I tell them that yes I do get tired of Ryan when he irritates me to death, I do get bored with him when he keeps on talking and talking and especially when I want him to shut up and my love for him has not at all remained the same since the time we have been together. In fact my love for him has grown deeper and more mature.

While standing in the balcony and thinking about all this I had another thought. There is no textual definition of love or being in love. When your mother does not sleep whole night just because you are suffering from cold, it is love. When a saint walks bare foot to the temple to offer flowers to the lord, it is love. When a small child cries just because his pet dog is not eating, it is also love.

Just like God is omnipresent, love is also present everywhere around us. Only we should be able identify it. In simple words love has different shades and each shade is special in its own way. Each shade fills the blogs of our life in different way and makes our lives colourful. Sometime it comes in the form of a lover and at times it is through friendship that we experience it. However, to love someone is one of the best feelings in the world and to be loved is one of the most beautiful blessings of the Lord.